Pignu ⸱⸱⸱⸱⸱⸱⸱⸱ ⸱ə

To Patricia
Best Wishes De,

a novel

by

Mifter Fool

Whereby
Jane Eyre meetf King Lear
on the ftormbound heath

Authored by

Def Dillon

This book is dedicated to my old Shakespeare lecturer and good friend David Jago for sorting out the these and thous for me.

About the Author

Des Dillon has won awards internationally for his writing. Born in Coatbridge, Scotland, he studied English Literature at Strathclyde University. Taught English. Writer-in-Residence at Castlemilk 1998-2000. Poet, short story writer, novelist, dramatist, TV scriptwriter and screen writer. His work has been published and performed in USA, Russia, Ukraine, Belgium, India, Sweden, Catalonia, France and Spain. Me and Ma Gal was included on the list of The 100 Greatest Ever Scottish Books.

NOVELS

Me an Ma Gal. (October 1995 by Argyll)

Duck. (July 1998 by Argyll)

Itchycooblue. (Feb 1999 by Headline Review)

Return of the Busby Babes. (2000 Headline Review)

The Big Q. (Feb 2001 by Headline Review)

Six Black Candles. (July 2002 by Headline Review)

The Blue Hen Novella. (spring 2004 by Sandstone Press)

Glasgow Dragon. (October 2004 by Luath Press)

My Epileptic Lurcher (Jan 2008 by Luath Press)

An Experiment in Compassion (March 2011 Luath Press)

Yelena's Leningrad (May 2015 by Seanchaidh Publishing)

Cunt: a true story. (March 2017 KDP)

Pignut&Nuncle. (December 2018 KDP)

SHORT STORY COLLECTIONS:
The Big Empty. (1997 by Argyll)
They Scream When You Kill Them. (2006 by Luath)

POETRY:
Sniz. (1994)
Picking Brambles, collection (2003 by Luath)
Scunnered, collection (2011 by Luath)
Love In A Modern World, a dozen love poems (KDP 2018)

STAGE:
The Bay for East (Glasgow Youth theatre. The Tron 2000)
Lockerbie 103 (Ashton Theatre. Toured Britain 2003)
Six Black Candles (The Royal Lyceum Edinburgh 2004)
Singin' I'm No' a Billy (Fringe Festival 2005)
Monks (The Royal Lyceum Edinburgh 2007)
The Blue Hen (Citizens Theatre Glasgow June 2010)
Billy an Tim an The Holy Ghost (Pavilion Glasgow 2015)

Contents

foolſ and kingſ and hurricanoeſ

A crack of lightning brights a blasted hazel within a ring of granite boulders. Even my teethre wet as I shiver in the pishing rain. Nuncles once powerful arms punch the heavens like a kryptonited Superman trying to take off. He roars Blow, winds, and crack your cheeks! Rage! Blow! & I pop rain outa my ears wi my pointers sos to hear better & hes like You cataracts and hurricanoes, spout till you have drench'd our steeples, drown'd the cocks!

He tilts up his head searching for the storms cause chokes & splutters on rain like a man drowning & retaliates by biting at it & goes You sulphurous and thought-executing fires! Vaunt-couriers to oak-cleaving thunderbolts, singe my white head! & he palmslaps his old grey bonce three times like a chimpanmonkeyzee.

Thunder answers wi a monstrous rumble & Nuncle drags his lips across his ample yellow gnashers & shouts And thou, all-shaking thunder, smite flat the thick rotundity o' the world! Crack nature's moulds, and germens spill at once, that make ingrateful man!

Lightnings taking photies of my foolish grin & warjet loud gusts offsuck shallow rooted trees into the universe. Terrified clouds panic & tumble the fuck outa here. Somethings goanny happen. I feel it in my toe bells. Somethings defo goanny happen man.

Then I see movement behind the veils of rain. I pop my eyes like a coke head & Jesus Christ shat myself a hare injumps & downflops gasping for air at our feet. Nuncle uppicks soft & backclaps gentle its ears & goes Is this the hare of whom the prophesy goes?

Say thee what, Nuncle?

This. This hare of portent; but yet I hope, I hope, it doth not point on me.

Prithee what doth thee bump thy gums about, Nuncle?

She dies of cold. See Fool.

He holds her to his breast for a girl she is & breathes warm over her nose. He lets out a wee squeak when one eye twitches & hes like Her eye stirs; she lives!

He stuffs her down his tunic till its just the ears sticking up & goes Haply you see a friend will save thy life. Nuncle smiles lightning kisses his teeth thunder slaps his ears & he gets back to ranting against the storm.

Thats when I see something else creeping the inky blasts. I nudge Nuncle & tell him but hes like I care not over someone lost. For indeed, I have lost command. That is more to care for.

Everybody is sometime lost Nuncle but some are unaware

they're lost and carry on regardless.

& as Nuncle attends to the hare by kissing her ear tips I splish splash ding splosh into the night to investigate.

The rain over my eyeball bends physics so that if some-ones out there theres more chance of finding a Catholic in the House of Parliament Orange Lodge. I stand still & let the rain make its applause on my roof but nothing stirs. Then light-ning lights an indistinct black shape a hundred yards away & I make my straight way over.

But I find myself back at the fuckin stones.

A flash photographs Nuncle tore & ragged wi the dead hare cradled in his hands. His face says wildman wolfman broken down oldman. I hide in a bush & watch over him. His popeyes are white whirling planets & in case they see me I furtherise into my bush. My rain varnished hands are photo-copied by fleeting moonlight.

Howl, howl, howl, howl! Nuncle goes O, you are men of stones. She's dead as earth.

I cough & he turns & shouts Fool? But I stay perfectly still & he shouts again Fool? Fool the Doe is dead! She must be buried as is our custom. Then he asides Wherefore art thou Fool? Ye slunk near as a teethy hound now blasted heath and biting storm abound.

The wind scatters debris & he takes two skelps of heather & one of thorn & shouts Fool me not in this wild and whip-ping hour. Show thy face to ice and rain and shower!

But a Fool has more to do than a King could ever know. He holds the Doe up by the ears to the Gods of grief & shouts

Ye Gods. Wert thou a man, thou wouldst have mercy on me & stumbles into the storm his rags a flapping shouting Fool! Thou lumpish pox riddled hedge-born rats-bane! We must bury the Doe boy!

When his voice & body are upswallowed I sneak from my hidingbush & take a breath of relief but then theres this other sound & I dive back in.

2

enter a woman

This woman late twenties or early thirties arrives like a sudden crisp poke on a gust of wind. A shawl slaps about her head & shoulders. Shes skinny as anorexias wee sister. She looks at the tree like she didnt expect a tree. She looks at the rocks & flings her palms out like what the puzzley fuck? Inspects the tree & circle of rocks. Then she speaks but not like me & not like Nuncle. This woman had a different spoke altogether.

North, south, east, west she goes pointing then scratches her head. I thought only characters in books comics & films done that but she actually scratches her coconut & confoundified goes North, south, east, west & inspects the tree again.

But I walked east she goes then ideafies Moss! she goes & finds moss on a rock then the tree & shes like Moss!

She fingerpoints and goes North!

I dont know if you know but moss grows on the north side of rocks & trees like a furry green carpet-compass. Theres always a way to find true north.

This woman takes a breath & her bearings & is about to walk off when she hears a robin chirping trouble. She finds it caged in a tangle of storm brush heather & twigs. She parts the prison wi grace & dexterity speaking soft words like bird poetry. Do not worry. I am not here to harm thee little bird. I am here to set thee free she goes & when the last straw cable is gone the robin jumps on her shoulder & chirrups twice & shes like Hello little friend. Fly. The whole world is yours now. But it bouncifies onto a branch & blink blinks & satisfied the bird is okay this woman checks her bearings & is about to take a step when she hears Nuncle shouting & stumbling in the murky swirl.

Fool. Be still he goes Do not desert me on this hill!

She softsteps back & listens.

I have buried the Doe boy! shouts Nuncle. The woman takes a step forward & shouts Hello? Out there? I am dire need of assistance! & off she squelches in the direction of Nuncles voice.

Shes gone a couple of seconds when Nuncle appears. He outsniggers when he realises hes back where he started & goes Ha! Trees do mock me wind and laughing rain. When walking straight's a circle, all's the same.

Hes patting the tree like an old friends back when the woman shouts faintly Hello!? Nuncle backjumps & goes Did thou speaketh rock?

But the woman shouts again she goes Out there! Hello?

Hark goes Nuncle in her direction Hark!

Can anyone hear me? goes the woman & Nuncle liplicks

& speaks into the squidblood night Goneril? My eldest born? Speak thee now! but theres no answer so he goes Second daughter, you, Regan sees sense thou? but theres no reply & he fullheights & shouts Fool! Is it thee out there? I am brainsicly. Come medicine me!

I feel grief expand in my chest enough to sorrowburst. I want to go to my Master my Captain my Nuncle my King but Foolrules have me stay cos the something I said was going to happen?

Its happening.

Medicine me. Medicine me, Fool he shouts & one dark step swallows him. His windfrailed voice cries Call, through the gale ye lifeless dog of hell. Laughing visage, nose and eyes show thyself.

& just when Nuncles voice is indistinguishable from the wind the woman steps through the stormwall places her palm on the hazel & makes a sound meaning what the very fuck is going on? She goes through her routine of inspecting the tree & the rocks then goes Sense dictates that I could not possibly have walked west and arrived east. All logic and philosophy and learning dictates this. I did not circumambulate fully around the earth so therefore this must be a different but very similar place. Yes this must be the explanation she goes but she doesnt believe her explanation. She believes shes back at the very same place. She thinks deeply then nods in agreement to an idea. She fills her pockets wi pebbles takes her bearings & heads into the storm dropping them Hansel & Gretel style as she comfortsings.

Wheear 'ast tha bin sin' ah saw thee, ah saw thee?

Wheear 'ast tha bin sin' ah saw thee?

On Ilkla Mooar baht 'at

On Ilkla Mooar baht 'at

On Ilkla Mooar baht 'at.

Zounds! says Nuncle appearing all of a suddenfuckly The King of tricks plays upon the King. Fie! Fie! Plays the Fool upon I this thing? Nay, he is neither brave nor sharp in brain, this magnitude of monstrous fake to feign.

Cheeky old cunt! This from the dunce who gave all his property & dosh to his two rottondotters so they could horse him into the storm wi no universal credit or pension. Just him & a wet Fool. Now hes daughterless soldierless powerless roofless friendless brainless & fuckin directionless wandering in circles in a storm.

Then he hears the singing.

On Ilkla Mooar baht 'at.

On Ilkla Mooar baht 'at.

Shush! he goes to nocunt in particular The wind language me in some strange song & when he eyedroplistens he sees a line of pebbles & goes What class of wind achieves a thing so neat as hand would lay these stones beneath my feet?

He stoops along the line collecting pebbles like a horseshit bagger.

Are these stones garments of Gods or of mind? he goes Showing worlds till now each was ever blind?

Then he hears footsteps & upright bolts & goes Hark something muttering this way comes! & he hides so close to me I can smell that stupid big white beard of his. Heres an arse coming towards him dropping stones Heavens he goes How hast this thing the gall to set its bum against the King?

He sneaks forward to the ring of rocks for a better look leaving his smelly fug behind.

Hark! whispers Nuncle What manner of back walk creature moves? What hair, cloth, neck, outlandish dress and shoes? Tis fit for shrouds or searing Spanish main. But storm? Nay! It stoops, it flings, it stands back up again.

He downducks as the woman recognises the stones & tree. If she was any good at swearing shed say aw for fucksakes but she lets out a teethy sigh then notices her interrupted line of pebbles & goes Hello? Is someone there? Hello?

It yawks in tongue of distant dialect goes Nuncle Whose tones and drones I yet… I'm apoplex'd.

The woman moves by chance toward Nuncles hidingrock. It comes says Nuncle leaning back & dissapearing into the gloom.

This cannot be. This cannot be she goes & one finger headscratches then sits on the selfsame rock. Her shoulders go up & down & I realise shes crying & muttering somebodys name.

Then sensing presence she twists & gloompeers. Nuncle

stillifies. Shes closer to Nuncle than a bee sting to its arse. She tucks deep in her shawl & lights a match. Nuncles twisted face appears in hideous yellow.

The woman screams.

3

nuncle & jane

& drops the match.

Nuncle screams.

She lifts a hefty handsize lump of granite Get back she goes Stand back Sir!

The match fizzles out on Nuncles busted boots & hes like What manner of flint is this!

She goes Get back I say! & sparks another match from the dry underside of the rock.

Tis a witch Nuncle goes From the cold stone sparks of fire do fly.

She raises the rock above her head & goes Who are you Sir? Nuncle inspects her like hes met a Martian in a pub toilet & goes Who are thee witch with clothes of a stranger stitch?

Hast thou been following me Sir?

Nuncle reaches out to touch her & she goes Do not touch me. I may be a woman Sir but I will strike you.

This is a woman I see before me? Thou art no woman afore seen to these eyes he goes & shes like I can assure Sir you I am a woman.

Nay nay goes Nuncle Thou art not. Nay nay nay & the angrified womans goes I am woman Sir, if thou art man. However, if I dared, I'd touch thee, to see if thou art substance or shadow.

But that thou was one thou too many for Nuncle & hes like Thou hast thoued me thrice, thou now ye me!

Pardon? she goes I have what you thrice?

Thou hast thoued me thrice, thou now ye me.

I have thoued you?

Yeah. Thou didst thou me thrice, when thou must ye me.

She tiny Mona Lisa smirks & goes I beg your pardon, Sir, but I don't know what you are talking about.

Tis good thou now you me. Ye forthwith bitch.

I beg your pardon, Sir! she goes Let me be plain, you insulted but Nuncleterrupts Good thou you me. Thou must you me forthwith & she sees madness in his peepers changes tack & goes I shall. I shall ye, or you, you forthwith.

Nuncle selfpoints & goes You herpoints & goes Thou then repeats the lesson for Ye & Thee.

I see goes the woman I understand. I shall ye and you ye as is your wish.

Thou never thou me when thou speaketh. Thou shalt serve out all respect I seeketh he goes Now what business hast thou with the King?

The king? she snorts like a Glasgow Ned & Nuncle nosealonglooks & goes What business with the King? Speak thou wench!

She releases a nervous laff & her knuckles tighten around the rock like a palepink wet crab.

Tickle not the King's catastrophe he goes Speak & shes like You are a king some kind?

Dost thou not feel the weight of royal gravitas?

No says the woman & he shouts Kneel!

I beg your pardon!

Kneel before your King!

Kneel? she goes On wet ground? Certainly not.

Kneel! he pointscreams.

I'm afraid my days of kneeling before men have come to a timely end, Sir.

Kneel I say! goes Nuncle grabbing her shoulder & fuck yi she clunks him on the boncebox & he backreels headholds & goes Argh! Argh! Argh! Rain diluted blood comes through the Vs in his fingers. Its like a moonlit advert for a Hammer House of Horror movie.

Stay away from me you madman! The woman goes high-holding the rock. Shes like a nightmarish Statue Of Liberty & Nuncle goes Do not stumble blind into regicide & inspects the blood in the lifelines of his palms.

I think perhaps I have stumbled into a lunatic she goes & Nuncle doesnt take too kindly to lunatic.

This starvelling eel-skin cries me lunatic? he says toward-stepping but she highholds the rock & goes Back Sir! Nuncle backsteps & asides She Sirs me well. But lunatics me too. Yet she's the lunatic of the two.

The woman looks around for A N other. I put that down

to coinkadink I mean – how the fuck could anybody except Gods & Fools hear asides?

Selene hath made her masterpiece in you Nuncle goes & shes like The words are real but in the confusion of accents, they make little sense & Nuncles like Question thou my oratory with guile? Whilst your squawking takes a while to compile & he songpersonates her On Ilkla Mooar baht 'at, On Ilkla Mooar & shes like I am leaving & Nuncle loudersings On Ilkla Mooar baht 'at, On Ilkla Mooar…

I am going she says Do you understand? Do not follow me.

On Ilkla Mooar baht 'at, On Ilkla Mooar baht 'at Nuncle sings & steps closer. She bares her teeth & goes I am a hard woman, Impossible to put off. Get back!

Theres a wee standoff then Nuncle shows his bloodied palms takes a step back relentsighs & goes Lay down thy rock, I am no danger to thee.

But this woman stays dangerous.

Lay down thy rock good woman goes Nuncle For in truth I am sickly, old, and unsure of things I see.

Were all unsure of the things we see even if were sure were sure of the things we see. I learnt that from Nuncle Immanuel. We need to pay more attention to what is real and what is not.

The woman looks at Nuncle the ground then Nuncle. She sighs into the whizz of the wind thinks for a second drops her arm & goes Are you alone Sir?

Alone? says Nuncle Yes. Here on this great stage of fools.

Are you lost on this moor Sir?

I cannot say true but these rocks and thon tree, wherefore I roam, repeat themselves to me.

Her eyes quickflash & she goes I have encountered similar circumstances in my attempt to cross this moor, Sir.

Sos to hear better I slithered through the bluedark bog on my back wi a Macbethbush covering my face & I got so close I ended up looking right up their beaks.

The woman goes When one walks away from this tree and these rocks, into the leafless shrubbery, no matter which direction one takes, one ends up back here?

Nuncle opens a happy hole in his face & goes You speaketh in a different language the same truth as I hath witnessed. Woman outlandish say where thoust has been.

I have been attempting to cross the moor in search of shelter, Sir she goes. As I walk, there are always great moors behind and on each hand of me, there are waves of mountains far beyond a deep valley at my feet. But I never seem to reach to the edge. And strangely, once I came upon these rocks and this tree, I seem to have lost all sense of direction. And now I find myself returning repeatedly to this spot.

Nuncle asides Tis strange, she speaks in witch's foreign tongue yet understand now I forthwith begin.

She peers into the dark & goes To whom are you speaking, Sir? & Nuncle eyebrow crunches & shes like Just there. You spoke. You said Tis strange, she speaks in almost foreign tongue etcetera, etcetera.

Thou… thou didst hear? goes Nuncle his eyes like snooker balls & the womans like Do you perhaps have a confederate in a hiding place nearby?

But I aside to the Gods goes Nuncle You cannot hear. Tis impossible.

I am stood very near, Sir. One cannot help but hear. Though I respectfully add I am not meaning to spy.

They are asides goes Nuncle Asides! Others are deaf to asides. Even evesdrypes cannot hear what Gods hear in aside.

I am no eavesdropper Sir. I can assure you.

Nuncle goes This madly mangled moor where all my strides return to this and women hear asides & he argh-frustrates & goes Why are you high upon this blasted heath strange woman?

Why are you come here Sir?

Answer firstly asked. Minion answers King he goes & shes like Yes I had forgotten you were king & Nuncle goes loudly Yeah!

Good evening your majesty she goes flinging in a wee contemptuous curtsy.

Nuncle handrolls his body length & goes Here's your Lord. Here's the King of all Britain. What say thee to that, Pignut!

If you will excuse your subject, your majesty she goes taking a cautious toefirst back But I must go now; and you should too: it darkens.

Whither too shalt thee go? If in circles thou dost tread?

I am going regardless she says her back leg disappearing into the stormwall as it would in deep vertical water.

Going? Leaving? Which? says Nuncle Lest it pull thee apart. Fox at a chicken or cheeks at a fart he goes & laughs &

she whips back red faced & goes I beg your pardon! & hes like The King's pardon is begged on one knee groundpointing & shes like I have been sentenced as a child to kneel a hundred times on a footstool and even so, I may indeed still go on one knee before a king, but a tramp and a madman? I will not Sir & shes surprised when Nuncle smiles & nods.

You smile incongruently, Sir she goes.

I have seen thou art ages with my youngest daughter and just as logger headed he goes & rainpeers Art thou she?

Am I who, Sir?

Art thou my youngest daughter come back from France?

She squints a wee bit before she goes I have no father or mother, brothers or sisters then she gawps at Nuncle like hes some kinda illusion trick or prank lets out a long breath & goes Goodbye Sir.

Goodmorrow then wench goes Nuncle waving one dismissive hand Let the storm take thee & she goes It has been a pleasure to make your acquaintance & is half disappeared into the stormwall when Nuncle shouts If thou dost meet two pestilent and foul daughters, do send them their father's bile

& at that the woman reconstitutes.

two pelican daughterſ

You have daughters? the woman goes & Nuncles like May the worm of conscience begnaw their souls.

In this vicinity? she goes You are saying you have daughters Sir, who are resided in this remote country?

I have nearby those who once were daughters.

But nearby? Two daughters close by?

Nay! Nuncle goes I have but one, whom thou dost remind me of. T'other two I cast off.

Glimpsing a tiny light of hope the woman goes These two, daughters or not, live near you say?

Live? Ha! Live? Live is a name fit for rats above these... daughters. Neither fit for that!

But could we seek shelter from cold and darkness there?

Shelter, wealth and power. They possess all! goes Nuncle & the woman headshakes & goes Then, Sir, these daughters are duty bound to provide their father with refuge in time of trouble. And, Sir, although a wanderer's repose or a sinner's reformation should never depend on a fellow-creature, I am hopeful these daughters may find the Christian charity in their hearts to provide shelter also for this lost soul in such a storm as this.

Fie, all the plagues that in the pendulous air hang fated o'er men's faults light on my daughters!

This is not the fashion in which a father should be speaking of his daughters she goes but that makes Nuncle madder & he lets rip wi They shall stand in fire to the voice and ice down to the eyes, so that offending part may burn and deceiving part may freeze.

Charming she goes I Sir have no father that I remember but I'd rather have none than a father who speaks of his daughters as you do. But I do see a certain justice in your losing all sense of direction.

I gave them all! Nuncle screams They tossed me down the pit of old age to live on spit and gall.

Nuncle stumbles suddenly & she automatically steadies him. The wind swishes a horrible gust & lightning crackles all around like a huge claw illuminating them in a grotesque living sculpture.

Thunder blastrolls & recedes. Its melancholy long withdrawing roar retreating down the edges & naked shingles of their minds leaving an eerie quiet into which the woman whispers But if you reasoned with them Sir, your daughters, on such a night…

Reason has been stripped back revealing ambition.

But on such a night, Sir!

I gave it all without suspicion goes Nuncle & shes like

Perhaps, Sir, perhaps if you informed me of where to search, I could locate your daughters and request shelter for myself and of course, for their father?

My daughters would turn ye to stocks or storm he goes Regan, Goneril and all of their swarm. Ha! They would pluck out your eyes.

Namecaught wi Shakespeare earworms her head jerks & she goes Regan and Goneril? & Nuncle goes They my daughters were. Now Cordelia & sheterrupts she goes Regan & Goneril? & he spits & goes Bile!

Cordelia?

France Nuncle says pointing to where France might be & he wouldve cried if the woman hadnt went Regan, Goneril, Cordelia? You are saying these are the names of your daughters?

Bury their names in boiling tar he goes Save sweet Cordelia.

And If one may be so bold to enquire, who are you Sir?

I have told thee he goes I am thy King.

Yes Sir, you have said, but if you could see a way to excuse my rudeness, what is your actual name?

Doth any here know me? he goes using his hands as the stagecurtains to his body Is this not Lear? he goes Doth not Lear walk thus? Speak? Are these not his eyes?

king lear iſnt real

The woman goes To be clear, for my head is in something of a spin tonight, Sir, due to recent events. You are saying, Sir, that you are King Lear?

Yeah! Sayest thou what to that Pignut? he goes & hed be as well saying Fuckin boom! or Fuck ye! The woman opens her mouth but her throat has been emptied of sense.

Observe and weep Nuncle goes King Lear! Say thee what to that? Baht 'at bum walker!

Say thee what to that? Say thee what? she points to the purple disc of the moon behind hurtling clouds & goes I say this to that Sir, that the moon has had its pull on you tonight. I say that you, Sir, are deluding yourself or making an attempt to delude me.

Delusion illusion or confusion reigns in thy tiny mind thou art losing. Hear this and tremble wench. I am thy King! he goes but she laughs & his blood reddens & he shouts I am thy King now tremble and obey!

Hes like thon Wizard of Oz turning that big dynamo handle & megaphoneroaring I am Oz the great and powerful! Aye right yar Oscar Zoroaster Phadrig Isaac Norman Henkel Emmannuel Ambroise Diggs. Sometimes we can just see right through to the other side.

King Lear? the woman goes & Nuncle puffs up to buffoonerymax Tastes golden on your tongue? he goes King Lear stands before thee in flesh and blood!

She bends over laffs straightens & goes King Lear, for your information Sir, isn't real.

Is not real?

Isn't real, Sir.

Either my notion weakens or my discernings are lethargied Nuncle goes circlewalking then he blurts out Ha! Walking? 'tis not so? Who art thou that canst tell me I am not?

King Lear is a fiction she goes.

My bones should melt then and my skin be rags to blow into the storm as vellum and dust should I be a fiction.

No she goes touching his shoulder *You* are real enough, Sir.

Make thy mind stick, for first I am fiction then real he goes boncepatting her Thy brains're filled with blacksmith's sparks and friction. I am what I am. No less and no more.

You are declaring your identity as King Lear?

Observe! Ye so thick as Tewkesbury mustard. This reality, this blasted heath, this storm, these rocks and trees, a dream of passion?

No. Not this she goes These stones, this tree, I am certain of their reality. Although they are, admittedly, somewhat strange.

Nuncle asides Somewhat strange since she arrived then remembers she asidehears & goes But she hears.

Yes, she hears. You have obviously read King Lear, Sir, and may I congratulate you, for you have read it well.

I have read myself as well as one man can.

I commend you on your choice also, for King Lear is one of the world's most revered fictions.

That appeals to Nuncles all but annihilated ego & hes like There exists a fiction of my own life wherein I had daughters three, rule and a wife? And bats brains to invent a life of strife?

Yes Sir and I am assuming you have read or watched it?

Watched my own life from without? Observe my own image? Ha! More of your conversation would infect my brain goes Nuncle & breaks a malleable branch makes a crown & goes On this great stage of fools. The King! This's a good block.

Perhaps where you previously dwelled you once saw it performed?

Dwelled? he grunts I did not dwell. I ruled. I ruled over all things he goes & armsweeps so wide she has to duck. She pops back up & goes May one ask a delicate question?

Ask wench you have been delicate thus far as an elephant.

Sometimes, sometimes, to entertain the patients, in an Asylum, the nurses will have a play performed but Nuncle doesnt understand & he headshakes.

A play! she goes mimeacting but hes still perplexed. On stage she goes picking up a propstone & going Alas, poor Yorick! I knew him, Horatio: a fellow of infinite jest, of most excellent fancy.

& Nuncle gets it.

Ah! Mummers and Rhymers and pace-eggers! he goes.

Yes! Yes! That's right. Mummers and Rhymers. Pace eggers.

Soulers galoshins and guysers?

Exactly Sir, a play, a drama, a performance, she goes & hes like You are saying King Lear, thou seest before thee, is a guyser?

I am saying, if one may be so bold, that you have watched these mummers and rhymers performing King Lear, and somehow, somehow Sir, it affected you such that now, or at some time in the past even, perhaps after some great personal catastrophe, you imagined, or came to believe, that you in fact are King Lear himself.

Nuncle backleans & goes I think I am King Lear? I *think* I am? & shes like Yes Sir & he goes Tis sensible to think thus as who I am is he.

Ah, I see goes the woman.

Clown to the left of him Daughters to right. Here he is stuck in the middle with you I sung to myself. I dont know why I came here tonight but Foolrules do.

I am King Lear Nuncle goes but she mistakes the grief in his tone for disbelief & goes You poor man! You have escaped. Or been abandoned.

Oh had I but escaped abandonment Nuncle goes.

Perhaps if we could find the way back to… wherever you were, she goes They, whoever they may be, could help. This is no night for anyone… mad or otherwise.

Nuncle after a long nosebreath goes Woman, since thou remindeth the King of his youngest daughter, I shall let you free without wager on thy head.

I could see a plan formatting in her eyes then goes I have a wager for thee Sir.

What's the wager?

If I could *prove* to you that King Lear is an actual play, Sir, a work of fiction, would you promise to lead me off this moor to shelter?

Ha! The King shalt wager six Barbary horses if thou canst prove. But what is thy end?

If I am deemed to have failed in my proof, I shall leave you to your fate Sir.

We'll make a solemn wager on your cunnings he goes & shes like May I have your word Sir?

Thou hast my word.

Im curled in a ball of darkness eager to see her persuade such a stubborn Nuncle. Ive had stubborn Nuncles before like Nuncle Rene. I told him he should go wi I am aware I think therefore I am but no would he fuck. He went wi I think therefore I am. Left hisself wide open.

The woman threads through the stones squelching but gathering her thoughts & muttering to herself. Then like a lawyer in an American courtroom turning suddenly to intimidate the witness she goes Immediately before King Lear arrived on this heath Goneril said he was getting old and weak and must give up half of his men.

The quick lights up in Nuncles eyes like Othello when Iago handed him Desdemonas hanky & shes like King Lear said he and his hundred men would stay with Regan but when pressed, Regan would allow only him twenty-five.

What monstrous stuff is this she jabbers? goes Nuncle astoundified.

Then what? the woman goes Then what? Ah! It is coming back to me. Yes. Yes that is it. Sir, so, on leaving Regan, King Lear turned his request back to Goneril, offering to reduce to fifty men. By now he was angry. Very angry.

Here were flickerations of fear. Nuncle strangetwisted his hands like Pontius Pilate wringing Jesus from his skin & went You were there or someone whispered thee this.

I can assure you Sir I was not *there* for *there* is not an actual place. In theatre, *there* is re-invented with each performance. I know what happened, Sir. You must ask yourself how this could be possible.

Nay! Nay he headshakes Nay!

I ask you to consider how it is possible that I know these things Sir? she goes & hes like The King's business is the chatter of the day down to the last uttered syllable. Thou hast been speaking with one who heard another tell sneer on smile what transpired, my loud applause and aves vehement!

As I have said already, I have met no-one on these moors, Sir, but you she goes & Nuncle stares hard trying to read the neurons synapses action potentials & neurotransmissions of her boncebox.

You have been elsewhere in your travels, nay? he goes &

shes like Yes I have and if you were to come with me to where I have been you might see, your mad-jesty, that the year is eighteen twenty-eight, not eight hundred and twenty-eight bc.

Mad-jesty man quality! Totally knicked for later Kings Queens Poets or Philosophers or wherever the Foolplanters nextstick me. Could be the future. Could be the past. Could be the present if we could ever find it.

Think! the woman goes How could I possibly know Sir, that Goneril was now no longer willing to allow her father, even fifty men and... and... Goneril and Regan were now acting as one against the King?

This flesh begot those Pelican daughters! goes Nuncle & eats rain gulpifying like a Pelican himself. Clump clump clump. When hes gulpless & breathless he goes Then what strange lady? How endeth this scenario?

With her hands on her hips she goes Goneril and Regan finally refused to allow King Lear *any* servants.

By Jupiter thou knowest, thou knowest & Nuncle now squelches in & out the rocks then goes Aha! Aha witch! The language they speak does thou know? Ah ha! You're caught he goes fingerpointing. You're caught! Rain runs off his nail.

But she goes Given some time, even though I may be paraphrasing at times, I might recall some of the lines, Sir, yes.

He doesnt know what paraphrasing means so he just goes Yeah?

Yes Sir!

Then proceed accordingly.

She thinks wi a finger crossing her lips then goes Hear me, my Lord; what need you five and twenty, ten, or five... to follow in a house... to follow in a house... where twice so many have orders... no command to tend you?

Gadzooks! goes Nuncle But how canst thou know? How canst thou know?

Because as I have repeatedly stated Sir, *King Lear* is a play!

But Nuncle is having none of it. He goes Regan! Say me more of Regan & the woman goes Lear was filled with rage. I cannot remember all of Regan's lines, Sir, but the end I do recall was something like this: You unnatural hags, I will have such revenges on you both... I will do such things... such things... what they are yet I know not: but they shall be the terrors of the earth. Something about weeping, oh yes... No, I'll not weep. I have full cause of weeping. And and... this heart shall break into a hundred thousand flaws or ere I'll weep. O Fool, I shall go mad!

Nuncle quietfalls but the woman continues she goes And at that point quite rightly outraged, King Lear, filled with anger, goes out into the storm with his Fool, whom you Sir, supposing for a moment that you are King Lear, seem to have misplaced in the meantime, although I suspect we shall never meet him.

I was tempted to shout Here Im here ya fuckin daftie but I bushpulled to morehide. Rain gurgled down my earhole & Nuncle stamped on my varnished hand as he paced about going How canst thou know? How canst thou know?

Because Sir, and I have to say I am becoming a little tired

of repeating this, because I have *read* and *studied* and indeed *taught*, in my position as a schoolmistress, a play by William Shakespeare by the name of The Tragedy Of King Lear.

Ah ha! goes Nuncle Ah ha! There are mighty gossips in my monarchy. Truth and liars employing some trick not worth an egg.

I have spoken to no-one from your *monarchy* Sir. I have met no-one on this moor but thee since I left Thornfield.

Aye aye he goes I knew a wench married in an afternoon as she went to the garden for parsley to stuff a rabbit; and so may you, wench. Get thee to a rabbitry with thy trickery.

She points & goes When Lear left Sir, Gloucester begged Goneril and Regan to bring him back inside, but they ordered the doors be shut and locked. How could I possibly know this?

Nuncle opens his mouth but she goes I shall tell you, because-it-is-from-a-play!

Ah! Silly-jeering idiots are thus with Kings! How could I know whatever thou dost know knowing not what was said behind closed doors? Rabbitry I say get thee hence, be fleet of foot. Go. Wish me insane no more.

It would be better for me if you were a sane and logical man she goes For I have no reason to lie.

Lovers, mothers fathers sons and daughters, all have reason to lie Nuncle goes & shes like I cannot communicate with you, Sir, for you are stubborn as a stone!

Kingdoms are builded on stones not on shifting sands Nuncle says & she fingerlips then asks Would you consider my position, Sir, if I could relate to you things known by King

Lear alone and so by logical extrapolation, if you have been exceptionally thorough in your assimilation of King Lear, known only by you?

Only by King Lear?

Yes Sir and supposing for a moment that you are actually King Lear, then you would have to question how I come to be in possession of such knowledge.

Ha! Witchery? Trickery? Mockery? Misery to mystery my history thou wouldst turn. But I am weary now with strife. Speak. My ears are open to thy madness. Entertain the lag end of my life. We'll begin that night I divided in three my kingdom's blight. Since mine own skull refuses to entertain me, I'll knock on yours he goes & domeclunks her. She goes Ah! boncerubs & goes Assuming, for the moment, that you are King Lear...

As I am.

Then Sir *you* decided to step down as King of Britain and divide your kingdom among your three daughters, Goneril, Regan and Cordelia, the largest portion of which would go to the daughter who loved you most.

Nuncle laughs & goes This too knoweth the kingdom and the cat.

You put your daughters through a test she goes Asking each the measure of their love & Nuncles like Well whistled by birds in trees. But proceed for the love of laughter.

Goneril and Regan gave replies fashioned to flatter parental egotism.

Pleased me well. Daughters set my heart aglow then let

me burn. But a donkey could bray these things he goes Say something that possibility thou couldst not know & the womans like Cordelia, your youngest and favourite, said only that she had no words to describe her love & Nuncle goes And witch, knowest thee the most exact words of Cordelia?

Yes I do the woman goes Cordelia said Nothing my Lord and King Lear, you, said, Nothing will come of nothing then.

Nuncles eyes bulged wi what looked like anger but we all know angers fear in a clanking suit of armour. Speak again witch he goes & shes like It has been such a long time since I have read the play, Sir she goes & Nuncle trunkpunches twigshiver raindropfall & shouts No Play! No Play. Speak again! Speak.

The woman puts up a polite hand & goes I will not bear continued outbreaks of your violent and unreasonable temper Sir & Nuncle tucks his hands in his tunic & goes Continue. Continue Cordelia's words.

Unhappy... the woman goes Unhappy that... I am... I cannot heave my heart into my mouth: I love your majesty according to my bond; nor more nor less. Yes this is exactly what Cordelia said.

Those are my Cordelia's words Nuncle goes Begads those are her words exact and true. Continue for here unfolds a replica, a life, a déjà vu & the woman does continue she goes You have begot me, bred me, loved me: I... Return those duties back as are right fit, fit... Obey you, love you, and most honour you. Why have my sisters husbands, if they say they love you all? When I wed... when I wed haply, when I shall wed, that Lord whose hand must take my plight shall carry half my love with him, half my care and duty... Sure, I shall never marry like my sisters, to love my father all.

Quietfalls Nuncle & into a stormpause the woman says I'm afraid King Lear flew into a rage Sir and banished Cordelia from his kingdom forever. Thus setting in motion a dark and melancholy tragedy.

Nuncle sploshes up & down considering the woman, considering the storms, considering his head inside & out, considering the fuckin lilies in beard stroking eye popping teeth clenching rain soaked consternation.

Then he spins & goes Hark Witch! If this be a play. If it be a play in thy head then middle beginning and end it must have?

Yes Sir as all plays do.

The he notices something about the woman an screams

out Ye Gods!

6

time & imagination

The woman goes What is wrong, Sir?

Ye Gods!

Sir?

Nuncle jawhang points at the womans watch & goes This... this drips as water on a castle sill & shes like My watch Sir?

Watch? And what does this watch watch? Nuncle goes & shes like It doesn't watch anything, it tells time & Nuncles like It hath an eye of glass and also hath a mouth to tell?

It doesn't speak, Sir, nor does it see. It measures time. It is a machine.

Machine? Machine? Nuncle goes Time's out of joint. Put it away! Cover it. Its monstrous eye doth vex me.

He clunks two sparky rocks three times going Fie, fie, fie, I say we crush it; let it go & she laffs like its the funniest thing shes ever seen & goes It is not an eye Sir. You wander, your head becomes confused. Has your malady caused you to forget clocks and watches?

She holds it up & goes It measures time but he laffsnorts Ha! Time hath no start nor end yet hath heft?

Record, records time.

Records?

Yes, she goes Records time yes, measures, records, past, present into future.

From our yesterdays to our dusty death?

Yes she goes In the end that's exactly what it will do. And beyond our dusty death too, and perhaps beyond the dusty death of the human soul.

Nuncle creeps forward in tiny steps. His eyes making a weird glassy triad wi the watch.

Drop the stones please she goes & thump thump the rocks go like closing cop car doors. Just missed me so I crawl deeper & sit like a mad boulder watching them.

Here, hold it she goes & Nuncle pulls his hands up like a praying mantis Nay he goes & shes like It's safe, hold it but hes like Nay! but fascination possesses his face & one hand makes a cup. She lowers the watch into his hand & covering it wi the mist of his grizzly breath Nuncles head follows the second hand. Like a boy wi a just caught finch he lets loose the tombstones of his mouth. When he places it to his ear his eyebrows rise in magical concentration.

Yet you tell me it drips out time he goes & she nods & hes like Drip drip drip. Doth this take my life away? Drip drip drip he goes & she headshakes & hes like Or do I gift it the power to pare? Do imagination and time share existence in this object?

Time shares existence in this watch, yes Sir she goes However I am not sure about imagination.

But time and imagination are bedfellows nay? he goes & shes like In what way are they connected, Sir? & he goes Perhaps not bedfellows. Hmm, imagination is the fishes that swim free through the nets of time.

I think you may be complicating matters Sir, for it merely measures time for one's convenience.

But Lears watchbound. He goes Speak, watch thing. Enchant the King with thy dripping whispers. Speak me Lear's future.

The woman takes the watch back and goes It is merely a mechanical instrument, Sir. It operates by Physics and scientific logic. It has no magic.

Then thou, witch with an extra eye, speak to me of Lear's future! What future becomes of Regan and Goneril? What of my lovely Cordelia?

I do not think, especially if you have indeed fully assimilated the character, that hearing of King Lear's future would confer any benefit on your condition, Sir.

Future me Nuncle goes & shes like In fact I fear it may have catastrophic consequences.

I demand this. Future me!

I cannot, will not, drive a fellow-creature to despair.

Ha ha thats ironic Im thinking & Nuncle goes Thou hath the King's word then witch. If thou relate me future scenarios, then on a King's promise, we shall retire to shelter.

You swear this Sir? she goes & hes like By Juno I swear. By

Jupiter I swear. By Apollo I swear. Begin with Cordelia.

You are certain?

Proceed Pignut.

You wish to know Cordelia's fate?

Proceed.

Im like Oh fuck I know where this is going & the woman takes a breath & goes In Dover a French army led by Cordelia lands with the intention of saving *you* & Nuncles like Cordelia? My dear Cordelia waft me 'cross the Channel?

No Sir.

No?

No Sir, she doesn't.

What then skinny one?

Cordelia does indeed land in Dover and you do see her, Sir, however…

Her words are in the mist but her porridge of knowledge is elsewhere cos she senses something moving in the dark. I think that might be me! I have to stop her telling Nuncle that Cordelia dies!

enter the fool

Someone approaches she goes & amazement fills her eyes when I crash into the scene wi my big stupid looking shoes one curled up & the other fell flat. Ting squelch ting squelch ting squelch.

Ting!

Nuncle armopens & goes Fool. Fool! There thou art following thy breath & Im like O Nuncle, court holy-water in a dry house is better than this rain-water out o' door.

There be magic Fool. This witch hath been prophesying what shall come to pass. I quickspin point & hee haw like a donkey & the woman goes Who might you be?

She had a good idea who the fuck I was but she didnt want to believe who the fuck I was cos if she believed who the fuck I was then it wasnt Nuncle who was mad mental crazy aff his bonce away wi the fuckin bongos. It was her.

I ask again, who are you Sir?

D'ye mean philosophy wise, existence wise in relation to otherwise empiricalized objects wise. Or subject as in I?

I am merely requesting, in all politeness that you provide

me with your name.

I am Fool. Some call me Fool but thou canst call me Fool.

Fool? she goes & Im like Fff ooo il cheeky cunt that I am

 but hey thats the job description ffs.

Your name is Fool? the woman goes.

The full Fool you fool. Fully understand?

I see she goes in that patronising voice doctors use when they talk to poor folks. I mean that part of the working class that sheared off in the nineteen eighties. That part that got left behind. The underclass that people above like to look down on grog on vomit all their failures on. Refugees but not in space - in time. Spacegoat scapegoats.

And if one may ask, Mister Fool, who is this man? the woman goes & Im like Who is who that is man to thee? & shes like This man here. Are you acquainted with him?

This man? He is he.

That he is he, is actually in question, Mister Fool. I am however enquiring simply as to the man's name?

That carbuncle mad eyed rain gulp swallower is my good Nuncle.

He is your Uncle?

All his other titles he hast given away, that he wast born with too, so we may call him carbuncle Nuncle all a funkle ding dong dunkle previously known as King. Dig a ling.

King? she goes And which king might your Uncle be?

So old and white as this. shouts Nuncle at the storm O! O! 'tis foul! & the rain coming down like long soft nails disappear into his eyballs.

Which king is he Mister Fool? she goes & even though I know who this woman is Foolrules serves me up cognitive dissonance so Im also thinking hold on who the fuck is she anyhow so I goes Who art thou maiden not so fair?

She doesnt pick up on the insult she just goes Jane & I go Well Jane-Jane thin and plain how didst thou come to the King?

I found him on the heath.

You were looking for a King, and how is luck with thee - you found one first time. Thou fall'st on him so luckily & shes about to speak when I interruptify Why were you looking for a King? Art thee short of a King in thy cunt – ree?

I wasn't looking for anyone, she goes I was… I was leaving… somewhere and then… then I found myself lost and whilst trying to regain my bearings I stumbled into… this poor man… in this dreadful condition.

Ah face of a crow and feet of a heavy hoofed horse neigh neigh neigh wonder she stumbled I goes & shes like I beg your pardon?

A King was lost but now is found by someone looking for no-one.

We are lost she goes & Im like I am not lost. For here I am! & she airhisses & goes Please stop this chattering nonsense &

I sails right into Nonsense makes no sense so I make some sense since you make enough sense of my nonsense to know that it is indeed nonsense & I shouts Nuncle come! Before Jane-Jane hoofs you deeper than oblivion with her thunder stumbles.

Come the King to where? he says To Perdition?

Good Nuncle, in, and ask thy daughters' blessing: come come. I shall lead you there, me the carrot you the hee haw hee haw hee haw. Don King Key.

Ah! goes Jane all enlightened all of a sudden Ah! Your arrival is making sense to me now Mister Fool she goes head-nodding. You she goes and pauses to nod at us one at a time Both have come from the same institution. You have both escaped from the same institution?

Yes. You are corright. From the same institution we come. Escaped the wrath of two women nuglier than thee pike face.

She ignores the insult an goes Do you agree with me, Mister Fool, that we really should find shelter from this wilderness?

Wilderness is everywhere about inside and out I go & she goes Sir, Mister *Lear,* one could perish out here. This man has just related to me that your *daughters* would give you shelter from the storm.

She shawlpulls the wool shining like leather in the wet & Nuncles like Ha! How canst a fiction perish prithee Jane?

A fiction, Nuncle? I go & he points a long dripping finger & goes From the thin and bloodless lips of stick hips cometh news thy King is a fiction.

Im like Strange Jane ye hath Nuncle carbuncle all in a fun-kle fiction? Tell a Fool of this & she goes I don't have him a fiction. He is… she reconsiders reconfigures & goes And not only he for it seems, Mister Fool, that you both are afflicted by the same malady.

Ha! See how she fictions thee also now boy! goes Nuncle & Im like Two little nutmegs sitting on a wall sire & he laughs & goes Doest thou know I am a part in a play by the title of King Lear boy?

And a long play, Sir, for my arse is sore these years being your audience of sometimes one.

A tragedy it seems.

Thou art suited well to tragedy Nuncle. Canst tell how an oyster makes his shell?

No boy.

Nor I neither; but I can tell why a snail has a house.

Why?

Why, to put his head in; not to give it away to his daughters and leave his horns without a case.

Lines from the play Jane goes You are quoting lines from the very play I cited, Mister Fool. It seems you have learned your lines as well as your Nuncle!

Sometimes a Fools jobs to confuse to the point of despair sos to break the shell between experience & actual reality. To force somekinda awakening. Ive been everywhere. In your life too you thats reading this. Ive avalanched you in absurdity so that you can be freed to clarity. Ive slaughtered you wi fool-ishness so you can be reborn to truth. My job is to blow the veil the fuck away. The worlds went too long on serious reason and went too wrong. Anyhoo... back to the tale.

This woman Nuncle seems as mad as to butter hay I goes & dancesings.

> She that has and a little tiny wit--
> With hey, ho, the wind and the rain,--
> Must make content with her fortunes fit,
> For the rain it raineth every day.

Nuncle sideslips & whispers She knoweth much that hath gone before. What was said even behind closed doors and claims to prophesy.

Perhaps she is mad enough to eat screaming snails Nuncle?

As mad as the vexed sea, singing aloud goes Nuncle & shes like I am not mad, Mister Fool, but may I suggest you two gentlemen conduct a close inspection of each other's claims to sanity?

I grab Nuncles beak & look down the blue tunnels of his eyes Nothing I go & shes like I find I have fallen into a great absurdity & Im like You have made Nuncle a fiction when he is real enough to slap your head till your jellies pop out.

I've had a mind to do thus this past time Nuncle goes outfogging at Jane & I goes Who did scribble you a life with their feathery quill Nuncle?

Some Shaking Spearing fellow he goes & Jane the pain goes Shakespeare. William Shakespeare wi the respect you save for Sprinsteen or Beethoven or Spielberg & I go Fullon-Fool Shakespeare I say Quivering trembling vibrating spear fellow doth well fleshing you to this Nuncle and did he magic this moor? Did he magic me? Every drop of rain fall from his quill? That rat bat dog and cat and even the arse where I shat? I sacrificed grammatical etiquette for rhyme.

Nuncle laughs deep & echoic like his whole bodys an empty shell.

Watch out for flying daggers Nuncle I go & hes like Some Shakespeare fellow made my toes and cock & I wank in Nuncles direction going Shakespeare. Shakespeare & Jane shockturns & goes How extraordinarily rude of you, Sir, you horrible little man!

She glares at me & if looks could kill all my ancestors would be dead.

Jane art thee real to breathe and feel like Nuncle and me or art thou too a fiction? I go & shes like I can assure you, Mister Fool, I am very real she goes & I go Yes and thus Nuncle is real & I outreach & tickle the mad old cunt till hes

going Tickle me not laff laff laff 😆 You would have me laugh here? We are in an improbable tragedy!

No Sir, you *imagine* you are in a tragedy she goes.

Ah! Ah! I goes Perhaps we three are fiction? Perhaps the whole world is fiction? Perhaps some Wavysword fellow dripped us all from his inky quill and we strut and fret all our days in quiet despair.

Ah ha! goes Nuncle outsputtering rainwater Dripped from his inky quill I like this one Fool, continue & I goes I say thou art a fiction hatchet face!

8

the fool fizzlef

Janes like How could I be a fiction Mister Fool? For I have just come to this moor from some… friends and some very real and adverse circumstances.

Jane Eyre I goes crashing the Foolrules & it **SIZZLES** me but I manage not to scream. She headswings left & right piousgrins & goes Ah. You almost fooled me. You have obviously been listening in the dark. Hiding out there somewhere on this desolate moor, listening to me.

Thou art used to shouting thine own name into the dark? I goes Lost thyself did thee? Looking for thyself and found a King?

I must have uttered my name somewhere, somehow and you, Mister Fool, were obviously close at hand to hear. Perhaps I used my name during prayer or was quietly muttering to myself as I ambulated, as one does.

A Fool can hear things in the dark as a wise man can see in light I says & we eyelock. By her unfocused gaze she is looking in as well as out. She downheadthinks then goes You would have infinite difficulty proving that I am a fiction Mister Fool, however, I could prove this man not to be King Lear and therefore, by logical extrapolation, you Sir, most certainly not to be King Lear's Fool.

Apollo plays with King and Fool alike I go Power to the flower of all petals. I see in I see out I see things I cannot speak about!

I see your strategy, I see it clearly. When placed under pressure speak in nonsensical riddles in the hope your opponent will weaken. Let me assure you I am not the type of woman to weaken, Sir.

This woman's not & easy glove, Nuncle I goes & he grunts his mind once again buried in the storm.

Jane goes They do say the mad are happily unaware of their malady. If you are not willing to seek shelter with this man's *daughters* then I shall leave you both to your fate and gamble with the storm but as she leavesteps Nuncle outblurts from his dwam We'll have proof! & Im like We will? & Jane goes And you shall honour to our wager?

I am a man of my word goes Nuncle We'll have proof.

And your Fool, well named I must say, will not interrupt?

I ducklip & Nuncle goes Let proof speak.

Jane reads some facts in the swirls of moonlight on the marsh grass. She soaks in whispers from the rain then cranks up her bright head looks straight at Nuncle & goes Think, Sir, and think hard she goes Canst thou, apologies, can you, recall further back in time than the day you divided your kingdom?

Yes, certainly Nuncle goes And doubt out of question too, and ambiguities.

Could you perhaps describe to me one of those times, Sir?

I can think of twenty times of better fortune goes Nuncle & shes like One will suffice, Sir.

Nuncle browdraws & sticks. I nudge his rib ladder going Nuncle? But his mouth moves & his lip trembles & his eyes pendulum. He upputs his head & goes Gadzooks! There's built a sudden moat around my recent actions & Jane flashes a sanctimonious smile goes Hmm then says Where were you born Sir?

Ah! goes a relieved Nuncle Ah! And at this time most easy 'tis to do't. I was born... I was born... Why my good stars. Forgot. I am weary; yea, my memory is tired. Have we no wine here?

But Jane wont let up. She goes after his weakness like a Yorkshire Terrier.

Have you any brothers, Sir? she goes

I...

Sisters?

'Tis in my memory lock'd.

What was your mother's name?

My mother...? My mother...? Nuncle goes nutscratching. (Yes those nuts) My mother...?

Perhaps you would prefer a less inhospitable question, Sir? she goes & hes like Yeah. Ask me easy. None that be wash'd in Lethe and forgotten.

& it was a good question Jane asked. An expert question. A fuckin cracker. I couldntve done better myself. Jees shes good.

What was your dead wife's name? she goes befuddling Nuncle & he armscratches & looks at me & I shrug & Jane goes Surely you couldn't have forgotten your wife's name Sir? & Nuncles like a chastised schoolboy before he blurts out The Queen!

Yes Sir, I am aware she is the Queen, however, I am asking whether she has an actual name?

Nuncle puts the index finger of his left hand in his mouth & once hes thunk he goes soliloquy silly hes like Of our too late deceas'd and dearest queen, whose soul I hope, possess'd of heavenly joys, doth ride in triumph 'mongst the cherubins & Jane goes He doesn't remember, Mister Fool & Im like give him time & she goes He doesn't remember because he has buried his own identity in oblivion and absorbed King Lear's identity as his own. And in King Lear, the play, one never hears uttered the name of the Queen. She is simply referred to as The Queen.

Nuncles mind is moated I shout You heard! Rains and pains and hurricanoes hath make him sick to forget that part of his life which was... bliss and blessed.

And in that part of his life, that is, the part of his life which lies outside the constraints of the Tragedy of King Lear, lies his true identity. In short, Mister Fool, this man is mad.

I pat Nuncle on the back & go What, art thou mad, old

fellow? & hes like all a panic O let me not be mad, not mad, sweet heaven!

And you Mister Fool Jane goes Either you are likewise mad or have some reason, good or ill, to profit from this poor man's condition and so make certain of prolonging your *Nuncle's* malady.

Nay. Nay. Thou hast me more a fox than a fool. I poke my master with spikes of love.

Thorns of love and roses of mirth goes Nuncle & she goes When, Mister Fool, did you first make acquaintance with *the king*? & Im like When we met that was the day I met him.

Which was when?

When? Why the day before the day after I met him to be exact and precise & I nearlaugh when Nuncle goes Tis true. Tis true. I remember the day well lovely boy. The birds did chant melody on every bush.

But Jane is getting exasperated infuriated just plain mad frustrated.

Where did you two meet Mister Fool? she goes & I'm like I beg your two fried eggs?

Where did *you* first acquaint this man who calls himself the *king*?

Why, in the place an inch from the place which is an inch from the place where we met.

True also goes Nuncle The King hath a genius for a Fool.

Jane ignores Nuncle & goes to me What is your name? & Im like Fool & she goes You have no other?

I answer to Fool sometimes Boy and sometimes a boot in

the arse. Call me Foolboy Arseboot.

Like thus goes Nuncle & boots me a cracker up the arse &
I kneedrop Argh! That hurt to the very brains this lady denies
us Nuncle.

Better soft padded bum as hard skulled head goes Nuncle
nodding at Jane but shes got more comebacks than Cliff Rich-
ard she goes Where were you born, Mister Fool?

Why - Atwixt my mother's legs I goes crotchgrabbing
& thrusting a Michael Jackson ooh! In her direction but she
ignores that & goes And your mother's name was? & I went
Maaaaaaaaaaaaammmy & Nuncle folds over hands on knees
& chokelaughs but Jane batters on relentless.

Do you have any brothers or sisters?

Half the world's my brother. T'other half my sister I go &
when shes thunk she goes Where were you on the day before
the King divided his kingdom? Fuckin boom! Another good
question. By fuck this womans good. But I just goes Why I
was where I always am.

Which is?

Right here inside my body pondering the reality of things
outside.

Her arms flop like wet spaghetti & she goes This is a
fruitless venture. You truly are a fool and this so called king is
more the fool than thee.

Aloof from th' entire point goes Nuncle Fool hear her?
& Im like I hear Nuncle, she tries to make thee a fiction and
fails so she turns her tiger on me. But her teeth are soft though
indelicate.

I think I have gone some way to prove the truth of the situation, namely that you have assimilated the identity of a fictional character, Sir. And this… Fool person, I fear may be involved in a web of mystification, the truth of which I have yet to ascertain. However, you Sir, have given your word, which I hope can be regarded as valid, that you would lead us to shelter.

My word is true Nuncle goes & shes like And yet here we still stand in the storm.

Nuncle will lead you to shelter Jane and sooner than thou thinkest I goes.

Clump thy gums boy goes Nuncle The King's word stands, Pignut, but I am not yet convinced. For if I am a fiction or a parody of a fiction why need I know grief? Anger? Rage! Why suffer, if my life no meaning hath before and none at end of my path?

Aye sometimes big daft Nuncle could get all sillysophical. Makes sense I mean how the fuck can a fiction feel grief? A reader can feel grief on behalf of a fiction but can a fiction feel grief? If they can then theyd exist. For real. They would actually fuckin exist! I remembered the words of Nuncle Pablo. Grief without shore.

Jane quietsaid If I could demonstrate to you, beyond certainty, that you are in fact not King Lear then this grief you claim to feel, Sir, would dissipate.

The grief is real goes Nuncle & he catches Janes eye & kazzom I feel her grief without shore too. So here we are ladies & mentalgents the bitter magnetic field of grief the poles of deep sorrow the magnetic flux of the crux of life has sucked these two characters out from ink & paper through that place we can never have knowledge of into existence on this heath this moor this plain of despair these ringing fuckin plains of windy Troy & even if Im the wooden horse theres fuck all I can do to help them understand. Ive been Foolruled & the punishments are dire.

Nuncles getting confused. He senses something should be happening. The engines revving but the brakesre on. He knows theres something he should be doing but cos Jane has arrived an upset the balance he cant work out what. &

I decide to distract Jane to give Nuncle the space so I go It seems thee art suited well to tragedy also Auntie.

I beg your pardon?

A King can pardon but if thou relishest the pardon of a Fool heres a fart for company I go & I coatlift & blast one in rotten egg stylee in her direction.

Once again how extraordinarily rude of you, Sir! I have had enough of this nonsense. I shall leave you two *gentlemen* to your fate.

She lifts her skirts to splosh off but Nuncle finds the thing he was looking for. His words. He screams out No, I will be the pattern of all patience; I will say nothing.

Lightning cracks nuclear white   thunder headpresses & we all downduck till it rolls away.

Then a voice from the shadow shouts Who's there?

9

ACT III SCENE II.

Another part of the heath. Storm ſtill.

Enter Kent

Out of the tempest trudges Lord Kent but hes disguised as Caius so that Nuncle doesnt recognise him. Jane eyebulges like shes seen the ghost of a ghost. Fool her once shame on Nuncle. Fool her twice shame on me. Fool her thrice what the fucks going on? Her eyes flick from me to Kent to Nuncle & her minds spinning like the reels on a fruit machine.

I give it my line Marry, here's grace and a cod-piece; that's a wise man and a fool & Kent goes to Nuncle Alas, Sir, are you here? Things that love night love not such nights as these; the wrathful skies gallow the very wanderers of the dark and make them keep their caves: since I was man, such sheets of fire, such bursts of horrid thunder but Janeterrupts wi I am sure you cherish your swelling spring of eloquence, Sir, but may I inquire if you have come from the same institution as these two gentlemen?

Whom or what is this creature? Kent goes & Nuncle opens his mouth but outcomes nothing so Kent looks stick hips up & down turns his back on her & goes Gracious my Lord, hard by here is a hovel; some friendship will it lend you 'gainst the tempest: repose you there.

Nuncle backslaps me & goes Come on, my boy: how dost, my boy? Art cold? I am cold myself. Where is this straw, my fellow?

Your gracious self goes Kent Embrace but my direction.

Mister Fool goes Jane Do you know this man? Why won't he acknowledge me? Who is this man?

Why this is our good Lord Kent I go & leaving Jane standing in KentCaiusstunned wonder I sing my wee song to Nuncle.

He that has and a little tiny wit--

With hey, ho, the wind and the rain,--

Must make content with his fortunes fit,

For the rain it raineth every day.

Nuncle goes True, my good boy. Come Sir, bring us to this hovel.

Thunder cracks lightning flashes clouds roll away from the moon & wi one giant Shakespearian Sonnet volta like step we arrive at the hovel or the hovel arrives at us.

10

ACT III SCENE IV.
The Heath. Before a hovel

Janes corkscrewing down into shock. She stares wide eyed at the hovel like a lost Pokémon. The stones of this dilapidated building have been rounded & smoothed by eons of wind & rain. The roof is boughs branches twigs & green moss. The door is rotten at the bottom like the ragged mouth of a wooden monster. Janes catching flies in her gub wi madstonishment as Kent aka Caius pushes open the door. It creaks like a rat steamrollered from tail to whisker & a darker darkness bleeds out filling the space around us & Janes mouth. She tastes that darkness & wrinkles her face.

Good my Lord, enter here goes Kent & Nuncles like Prithee, go in thyself: seek thine own ease but Kent doesnt move & Nuncle goes to me In, boy; go first but before I can move theres a noise.

Jane fearsteps behind Nuncle & Im like I'll go in first after thee go in first Nuncle.

Nay, get thee in he goes I'll pray.

But, there's something in there lurking Nuncle.

I am thy King! In boy Nuncle goes & boots me sore as fuck up the arse. As you can probably tell he likes dishing out boots up the arse. I limp hand on arsebone dustdragging my damp shoe bells for the earthen floor is dry. The door squeals closed like an unsteamrollered rat whisker to tail. I inbreathe & peer around. Shapes & shadows forming. It feels like the hovel is filled wi images.

Fathom and half, fathom and half! Poor Tom! says a voice. Fuckin shat myself! I jumps so high my bells dry out & ting in the pause at the top. Im like Wile E Coyote as I try reach the door arms & legs going in thin air before I hit the ground but the ghoul grabs my arm so I shout Come not in here Nuncle. Here's a spirit & the spectres pulling my arm hand over fist down his ghostly breath to the very jaws of hell.

O strange! I go We are haunted. Pray, Nuncle! Fly, Nuncle! Help! Nay run! & thats when Kent crashes in sword drawn & goes Who's there?

A spirit I shout A spirit. It says its name's poor Tom.

Kent goes What art thou that dost grumble there i' the straw?

This *thing* steps into the doorway moonlight stark fuckin bollox naked & once I can take my eyes off his hing for a big hing it is I realise its Edgar in disguise. Edgar playing the madman to avoid the law & playing it rather well I have to say for theres not a lot of men in the kingdom could go about wi their dick hanging out & no smirk on their face be it the smirk of pride or the smirk of shame.

Could a lady request that you please cover yourself, Sir goes Jane turning to the storm.

Nuncle doesnt realise its Gloucesters son Edgar but he empathises wi the madness in Poor Tom & thinking hes also been turfed out on his arse by his daughters he goes Hast thou given all to thy two daughters and art thou come to this?

Who gives anything to poor Tom whom the foul fiend hath led through fire and through flame? Bless thy five wits! Tom's a-cold. O, do de, do de, do de.

& Tom gives a wee sane squint at Janes strangeness & I see question marks float over his peepers but he snaps back to his madness immediately.

Is man no more than this? goes Nuncle Consider well & he disrags to donate his clothes to Poor Tom & Im like Prithee, Nuncle, be contented; 'tis a naughty night to swim in but soon theres two ding a lings hanging in the cold wet night & I have to state for the record that Nuncles dong seems to have lost size & girth since his rottendotters humiliated him. This was the dick of a ruined man. More skin than bone. Nuncle dresses Poor Tom going What, have his daughters brought him to this pass? Couldst thou save nothing? Didst thou give them all?

He hath no daughters, Sir goes Kent & Nuncles like He hath no daughters?

He is a Tom a Bedlam, Lord.

Pillicock sat on Pillicock-hill: Halloo, halloo, loo, loo!

Nuncle ushers Poor Tom further into the hovel going In,

fellow, there, into the hovel: keep thee warm & thats when I spot over Nuncles bare shoulder the flicker of an approaching torch in the storm.

Look, here comes a walking fire I go & the side of Gloucesters face is lit a lurid red as he approaches. By this time Janes so shocked she vomits on the straw. Gloucester bends to come through the doorway outholding the torch. I spit smokesmell & flametaste. First thing he sees are dancing flames on Poor Tom & goes I mistook thee for my son. For a moment thou wert his image.

Poor Toms a cold! Poor Tom's a cold! Goes Tom & Gloucesters like But thee art less the monster than that abhorred villain! Unnatural, detested, brutish villain! worse than brutish!

I thought I saw Poor Tom gulp.

Gloucester throws the light of his torch on Kent and goes Begads! Thee Sir have the likeness of another man I know. A good man banished for the offence of honesty. Ah! This night hath a man more puzzled than the Egyptians in their fog & at that he swings his torch to Jane. Her jaw hinges open. Her logic has disintegrated. Her words are stuck to the inside of her cheeks like a packet of cream crackers wi no milk. Were all so certain others are wrong in the things were certain of. But sometimes when we jump into water we jump into the abyss.

Come speak, outlandish… *thing* Gloucester goes Where is the King my master?

Jane nods & Gloucesters torch finds Nuncle & he goes My Lord I ventured to come seek you out, and bring you where both fire and food is ready.

Poor Toms a cold! Poor Tom's a cold!

Come to shelter your grace goes Gloucester & throws his cloak around Nuncles shivering body.

Theres a pause before Nuncle speaks. Poor Tom eye bulges the rafters. Gloucester observes his masters lips. Kent fiddles wi his buttons to keep his face hidden & Jane desperately breathes in & out.

Come, good Athenian says Nuncle.

Lightning.   Thunder.

II

ACT III SCENE VI. A chamber in a farmhoufe adjoining the caftle.

Fuckyi! I arseland in Gloucesters farm & Janes standing benumbed in the straw. Nuncle blows warm air into Poor Toms icy hands.

Poor Tom's a cold. Poor Tom's a cold.

I know what I have to do.

I produce two sheeps heads from a shabby wooden box & go Ah ha! Sheeps heads Nuncle! & I hold one aloft & go Regan then the other & go Goneril! The accused Nuncle!

A trial! Good boy! A trial! Sheeps heads for representation of the Pelicans. We shall have a trial! I will arraign them straight. Come, Poor Tom, sit thou here, most learned justice.

Poor Tom's a cold!

Poor Janes astonished.

Nuncle claps his hands twice & goes Bring in the evidence.

I hold up Goneril baaad & hes like Thou robed man of justice, take thy place & I place her on a shovel & Nuncles like

And thou, her yoke-fellow of equity & I place Regan baaad on a rake.

Nuncle, time has made your daughters prettier I go & kiss each head.

 Mwah!   Mwah!

Strands of bloodied wool stick to my lips.

Arraign her first; 'tis Goneril Nuncle goes I here take my oath before this honourable assembly, she kicked the poor King her father & he stands up to show us his bruised shin.

Come hither, mistress I go Is thy name Goneril? & Nuncles like She cannot deny it & Im like Cry you mercy, I took you for a joint-stool.

Nuncle Laffs. Poor Tom laffs. Jane doesnt.

By the time the trials over Janes numbness is wearing off. Nuncle goes Make no noise, make no noise; draw the curtains & falls asleep in a dryshit cowstall & Im like And I'll go to bed at noon & then Gloucester crashes in all a fluster gasping for breath & goes Good friend, I prithee, take the King in thy arms; I have o'erheard a plot of death upon him. There is a litter ready; lay him in't, and drive towards Dover.

Somewhere in the cracks of light & hammer blows of thunder

I hear Jane rationalising she goes I am having the most frightful nightmare.

ACT IV SCENE VI. Fieldſ near Do ver. Enter KING LEAR, fantaſti cally dreſſed with wild flowerſ

This time I scud my arsebone on a white stone that says Dover Six Miles & I screamdance as a warm breeze weaves poetry in the long grass of the flower pocked slopes. As the pain subsides a bewilderified Jane appears. The sun is hot & sweat beads sparkle on her forehead.

Mister Fool what is the explanation for this? Am I dreaming? she goes & I give it fullfoolshrug & she goes This is all so strange and dreadful to me.

Nuncle comes a prancing down a grassy knoll wi flowers in his hair & his body decorated wi grasses twigs & things of the earth never before used as clothes. I think of If youre going to San Francisco be sure to wear some flowers in your hair but obviously canny sing it out loud.

Your majesty, Mister Lear, stop. Stop! Jane shouts intimidated by the grinspinning King. Nuncle doesnt recognise her.

He doesnt even know shes there so she stops him by both-handing his shoulders & goes It's Jane.

Ha, 'twas a merry night! And is Jane, Jane?

Jane, Jane Eyre, the farmhouse, the hovel, the storm! Don't you recognise me? she goes a creaking note of panic in her voice.

Where's my Fool? Nuncle goes Ho! I think the world's asleep & plumps his ample arse beneath a tree wi five leaves like the one Godot planted & nocunt knew what for. Then out of a mysterious wee swirl of summer sea haar this old man wanders & by the way hes holding his hands out I see hes blind. He bumps into Jane & she yelps at his outgouged eyes crusted wi puss & blood but I could tell her yelp wasnt just for the outgouged eyes.

 Gloucester? she goes My God! Gloucester!

Who goes there? Gloucester says inching forward in grunts & nasal breaths. His fingertips tremble over Janes face & she goes A friend. It is a friend before you.

I know that voice friend.

I am Jane Eyre. We met at the hovel. At your farmhouse.

Good woman, canst thoust help an old man? Canst thou lead me to my King?

I can Sir and I shall.

Apollo bless King Lear Gloucester goes & Jane step by steps him to Nuncle who is singing a happy ditty to a daisy chain in the dappled shade of an oak.

Your majesty you have a visitor she goes & Gloucester blunders forward like a drunk bear finds Nuncles wrist & goes

O, let me kiss that hand! but Nuncle pulls it back & goes Let me wipe it first; it smells of mortality.

He wipes it on the grass like a battered fish one side then the other & offers it to Gloucester. On the kiss electric currents of grief surge through Gloucesters lips & black tears of tar outcome his blood crusted sockets & a long wail comes out & he goes O ruin'd piece of nature! This great world shall so wear out to nought. My Lord dost thou know me? Dost thou know me Lord?

Nuncle massages Gloucesters ravaged hands & goes I remember thine eyes well enough.

Alack! Alack the day goes Gloucester & for some reason like & Alzheimers sufferer hearing & old love song Nuncle lifesparks to a clarity that fades as he speaks. He turns to us all & goes When we are born, we cry that we are come to this great stage of fools: this a good block; it were a delicate stratagem, to shoe a troop of horse with felt: I'll put't in proof; and when I have stol'n upon these sons-in-law, then, kill, kill, kill, kill, kill, kill!

Nuncle swings an air sword killing the soldiers of his mind just missing blind Gloucester twice & Jane once wi his fists in the process. The breeze gets up goes Gloucester sniffing at sweet traces of summer in the air.

Jane headwhips to the grassy knoll as a Gentleman & two suited booted & well groomed Attendants income. They upstroll to Nuncle & the Gentleman goes O, here he is: lay hand upon him.

Nuncle starts & the Gentleman goes Prithee peace Sir, for

your most dear daughter but Nuncle goes Nay, if you get it, you shall get it with running & he bolts shouting Sa, sa, sa, sa wi the Gentleman & one Attendant bounding after him.

I turn to speak to Jane but Im turned into electric milk by a bolt of lightning. I raise my hand against blinding light &...

ACT IV SCENE VII. A tent in the French camp. LEAR on a bed afleep

Cordelia constitutes out of the light. She gawps at Janes clothes & goes In God's name, what art thou?

Jane gathering her wits wi her breath & goes I am a faithful servant of the King, good Cordelia & Cordelia nods to her father attended by a doctor & goes My name, servant, is hateful to myself.

Your name should not be hateful, for your father loves you more than you can imagine.

Cordelia uppicks the daisy chain Nuncle filled wi happy songs & a wee bit distant she goes He made thus when I wert a child. How does my royal Lord? & Jane goes He sleeps for now. But when he wakes I fear he shall not know me, and perhaps not you.

A father shalt not know his daughter?

I am afraid, Cordelia, that his mind has broken down with grief.

Cordelia falls still as a winter rock so that Janes got to touch her hand to undwam her. Cordelia flinches & Jane goes I must implore you Cordelia to take your father and flee to France.

Flee? To France?

Yes immediately.

Why to France with the King almost restored?

To save your life and the King's. There is immediate danger.

Art thee mad as thy clowns apparel?

Cordelia, a sense of terror confuses my faculties so that I cannot properly explain but if you could find it in your heart to trust a well meaning stranger, that trust would be rewarded tenfold.

Ha! goes Cordelia Ha! These hands itch to repair those violent harms that my two sisters have made! I make war with womankind & she returns to Nuncles sick bed.

And if you are defeated? Jane goes & Cordelia whips her head round & goes defeated? God's peace! I will not lose so just a war & as Cordelia strokes her fathers head in the overbearing silence Jane gasps There have been portents.

Portents? Cordelia goes & Janes like Portents are strange things! A mystery to which humanity has not yet found the key.

What are these portents?

Portents, which perplex and pain me to relate, of coming tragedy.

Cordelia stands face to face wi Jane & goes Thoust knows

of a portent?

Jane nods aye.

Speak then this portent clown goes Cordelia but Janes reticent till Cordelia roars Speak! & Janes like There are portents that you would be defeated by your sisters, captured and put to death and as result of this, your father will die of grief.

Jesus Christ dont hold back Jane for fucksakes! Theres a metallic slicing sound as Cordelia draws her blade & goes Blood would I draw on thee – thou art a witch but Jane backsteps & goes I'll say no more. Be at peace, Cordelia!

But Cordelia goes Mine true love for my father shall assure revenge. She halfsmiles holds the sword point to Janes neck & goes What ills my father?

You must be prepared goes Jane Your father has changed since last you saw him.

How changed?

I cannot say exactly.

Wake him Physic goes Cordelia holding Jane on the sword like some kinda dug on a steel leash.

The Doctor goes Madam, do you 'tis fittest & Cordelia overleans Nuncle blows on his face till his eyes flicker & goes How does my royal Lord? How fares your majesty?

Nuncle brainforms Cordeila & goes You do me wrong to take me out o' the grave. Thou art a soul in bliss; but I am bound upon a wheel of fire, that mine own tears do scald like moulten lead.

Sir, do you know me? goes Cordelia & Nuncle sits up wi his palms on the grass blinks blinks again & goes You are a spirit, I know. When did you die?

He is still, still, far wide! goes Cordelia.

Where have I been? goes Nuncle Where am I? Fair daylight?

O, look upon me, Sir, and hold your hands in benediction o'er me goes Cordelia & Nuncle headtilts & goes I fear I am not in perfect mind. Methinks I should know this girl & Janes like Look at the girl, Sir. Who is she? But he points at Jane & goes And I should know this woman.

Jane & Cordelia lookshare & Nuncle goes What place this is? Where did I lodge last night? Then his eyes settle again on Cordelia the clarity returns & he goes Do not laugh at me for, as I am a man, I think this lady to be my child Cordelia.

And so I am, I am. Look upon me, Sir, and hold your hands in benediction o'er me.

Nuncle kneels before Cordelia like shes a goddess.

No, Sir, you must not kneel & Nuncle upreaches going Be your tears wet? Yes, 'faith. I pray, weep not. If you have poison for me, I will drink it.

My King shall drink to victory's sweet breath goes Cordelia & hes like Am I in France?

He runs his fingertips across the grass & tastes the dew & Cordelias like In your own kingdom, Sir.

Do not abuse me he goes smacking his lips The dew tastes of France.

You are in your own kingdom my good Lord she goes & helps Nuncle to his feet saying Will't please your highness walk? Nuncle limps off wi Cordelia. His voice bellowish &

powerful against the storm is feeblified as he croaks You must bear with me. Pray you now, forget and forgive: I am old and foolish.

Janes wits are pulling together cos she goes Exit Lear and Cordelia but before she can utter a half a syllable more theres lightning. Thunder.

Electric milk. Bzzz bzzz & all is abruptly dark. I feel us being elevated. Then were rolling through clouds.

ACT V SCENE II. A field be
tween the two campſ.

Alarum within. Enter, with drum and colourſ, KING LEAR, CORDE
LIA, and Soldierſ, over the ſtage; and exeunt

Flying through the sky way way above the earth. Janes screaming like a wane on the wrong roller coaster. Then far below Nuncle Cordelia & the French army march to war. Theres the dreadful sounds of drumming hoofs metal on armour tearing skin wailing boys beating hearts rasping final breaths & squirting blood.

Then the void & the muffled   of
thunder & lightning.

15

ACT V SCENE III. The Brit
ifh camp near Dover.

Enter, in conqueſt, with drum and colourſ, EDMUND, KING LEAR
and CORDELIA, priſonerſ; Captain, Soldierſ, & c

I peer through a tentflap like a cat through dog infested fence. Inside seasound soothed Cordelia is chained to Nuncle & Nuncle is chained to Jane. Nuncle grinlistens to the moons story.

Cordelia rattles her chains sending a sine wave to Jane an goes Ah, thou art a witch to prophesy so! Jane has black circles round her eyes & a wee tough sneer at the side of her lip. She goes This, if it was made and isn't some dream, some vision from another world, was made so, Cordelia, by your father's pride and by your own silence.

This silence for my sin you dare impute?

Yes! I do dare impute.

Yes?

Yes.

Prithee explain witch!

You should have told your father you loved him.

I have, from these lips and you have seen.

Not now. Not the last scene. You should have told this to him in act one scene one!

Cordelia starepuzzles & goes Where are these acts and scenes of which thou dost mutter?

I am speaking of the day your father divided his kingdom. You should have told him then you loved him fondly.

I did as thou sayest goes Cordelia.

No. No, you did not Jane goes Your frivolous and childish pride prevented you from embellishing your words as did your sisters.

Cordelia stares at Jane through her eyebrows & goes I did as was fit to do.

If you hadn't been so bound by your naive pride Jane goes Then it is highly probable none of this could have happened. It would be, in fact, in my confirmed opinion, utterly impossible. Now, Cordelia, I am afraid you must rally your forces for the worst.

Before Cordelia can reply Gloucesters power hungry son Edmund inmarches wi four officers. Take them away good guard he goes & Cordelia goes to Jane We are not the first who, with best meaning, have incurr'd the worst & she goes to Nuncle For thee, oppressed King, am I cast down. Myself could else out-frown false fortune's frown.

Jane tries to resist but is booted in the face & falls wi a squeal & a bloody lip. Outside Cordelias head scans for Regan

& Goneril. When she cant find them her mouth twists in rage & she sneers to Nuncle Shall we not see these daughters and these sisters?

But Nuncle huddles into her like a junkie going home wi a score & goes No, no, no, no! Come, let's away to prison. We two alone will sing like birds i' the cage & before Cordelia can answer Edmund shouts Take them away & the guards drag them off.

I become all sorts of crazy rat cat & bat shadows following Nuncles summer night-time voice at a safe distance. I skitter sideways at an angle past posts guards trees & sentries catching glimpses of Nuncles burnt-out hulk moving through the barcode of the trees.

When thou dost ask me blessing Nuncle goes to Cordelia I'll kneel down and ask of thee forgiveness so we'll live, and pray, and sing, and tell old tales, and laugh at gilded butterflies, and hear poor rogues talk of court news; and we'll talk with them too. Who loses and who wins; who's in, who's out; and take upon's the mystery of things, as if we were God's spies: and we'll wear out, In a wall'd prison, packs and sects of great ones, that ebb and flow by the moon.

But Cordelia has been dragged away in the direction of a lone hazel & its twenty more steps before Nuncle swings in panic & hollers Cordelia? Cordelia? Where art thou Cordelia?

She has gone, Sir goes Jane They have taken her away.

Away?

Yes Sir. In that direction. Whilst you were speaking.

Upon such sacrifices goes Nuncle My Cordelia, the Gods

themselves throw incense. He that parts us shall bring a brand from heaven, and fire us hence like foxes. Wipe thine eyes. The good-years shall devour them, flesh and fell, ere they shall make us weep: we'll see 'em starve first. Come.

Lightning cracks.

Thunder blasts. We tumble.

16

ACT V SCENE III. The Britifh camp near Dover. Reenter KING LEAR, with CORDELIA dead in hif armf

Nuncle lays a limp Cordelia on the warm evening grass.

She's dead as earth he goes Lend me a looking-glass. If that her breath will mist or stain the stone, why, then she lives.

I have none Nuncle I go but Jane takes out the watch & goes This has glass on the front Sir.

Nuncle holds the ticking eye to Cordelias mouth & goes The air breathes upon this glass here most sweetly.

I think that may be from your own breath, Sir Jane goes & hes like Nay, Nay & holds a white feather to Cordelias lips. Concentrating on the edges of the vanes he gasps & goes This feather stirs; she lives! If it be so it is a chance which does redeem all sorrows that ever I have felt.

Theres a silence of indeterminable length before Jane goes Your majesty I fear she is gone.

Gone?

Yes your majesty, passed over.

Nuncles eyes squint. He lets out a whine & goes A plague upon you, murderers, traitors all! I might have saved her; now she's gone for ever!

He scoops her in his arms & goes Cordelia, Cordelia! stay a little.

Air expels from her throat & Nuncle goes Ha! What is't thou say'st? but her head flops & he pulls her to his chest & goes Her voice was ever soft, gentle, and low, an excellent thing in woman.

Yes. Yes it is, Sir. A most excellent thing.

I kill'd the slave that was a-hanging thee.

'Tis true, my Lord I goes You did.

Did I not, fellow?

You did Sir goes Jane You killed him.

I have seen the day, with my good biting falchion I would have made them skip. I am old now and these same crosses spoil me. Who are you?

Jane Sir.

Mine eyes are not o' the best.

Jane shifts some strands of hair from Cordelias dead & staring eye & goes She loved you, Sir.

Who are you? Remind me.

Jane Eyre she goes but he blanklooks & shes like We met on the heath? In the storm?

This is a dull sight he goes turns to me & goes Are you not Kent?

No, my good Lord; I am not Kent. He is with Albany.

Never the less you are welcome hither, tell me what the day hath done to my Pelican daughters. The hour destroy them?

Yes Sir, Goneril and Regan are dead.

I should rejoice now at this happy news but now my sight fails, and my brain is giddy. O me! Come near me now I am much ill Nuncle goes & squeezes Cordelias body & Jane wants to make a move of comfort but cant.

And my poor Fool is hang'd! & Im like what the fucks he on about Im right here he just fuckin spoke to me but I get the fear & feel my neck for a rope in case Im already dead & I shite myself when Nuncle screams & takes Cordelias face in his hands & goes No, no, no life! Why should a dog, a horse, a rat, have life, and thou no breath at all? Thou'lt come no more, never, never, never, never, never! Pray you, undo this button: thank you, Jane. Do you see this?

See what, Sir?

Look on her, look, her lips & Jane looks & goes I can't see…

Look there, look there! goes Nuncle & floorslumps dead & the world fills wi lightning. The whole actual world. All is white. & a terrible thunder comes behind it.

returned to the heath(1)

We crash back onto the heath. Nuncle crouchs over Cordelias body but shes melted like wanny they dreams when you try to drag something from dreamland into the morning but wake wi empty hands & the hollow sense of loss. Nuncle collapses into himself & I sit in his puddle & stroke his hair. Hes my wolfhound now.

Bedraggled Janes muttering rationalisations as to how all this could be. How she had left Thornfield & wandered onto the moor & slept one night & walked the next day straight into a storm & became became became so lost that she repeatedly arrived back at the same spot & then met this this this King Lear & was sure he was an escaped lunatic but then his Fool turned up & then... then...

None of it is making any fuckin sense but her hands are doing the sums & her fingertips are feeling for a grain of salt in the sea.

I lean to Nuncles ear & tell him a wee story to soothe his sobbing.

Once upon a time Nuncle, there was a room in an attic where a man didst lock his mad wife, for a dangerous woman she be. Canst thou hear me Nuncle? Locked her in & attic! Is this a good block? Nay? But there's more.

This man, this **Rochester**, had a mistress Nuncle, who didn't know of this mad wife in the attic. (By now the **SIZZLE** was starting so I knew Jane was listening) And being a woman of iron clad principles, rules, laws, ethics, morals and societies' values this mistress, when she discovered and uncovered the man's wife in the attic, blubbered and ran off in wholly the wrong direction, as we are wont to do at certain times of our lives and soon she found herself lost on a dark and stormy heath.

The **SIZZLE** was too sore now so I goes Art thou listening Nuncle?

& Janes like No but I am listening Sir and wish to know just how you come to be in possession of this information regarding my past life? & I goes Midway through this life we're bound upon I find myself in the middle of a dark moor with the road out wholly lost or gone.

Mister Fool Jane goes Considering what we've recently been through, whatever that may have been, dream, hallucination or some otherworldly reality, I think you are duty bound to answer my question with something other than a well-known and oft repeated verse of Dante's Inferno.

Duty, morality, principle miss piss, it's all nonsense I goes Nuncle prick up thine ears for the story continues and thee canst list as the night time hazel listens to the passing hind.

Anger flares in Janes eyes & theres a wee twitch of the shoulder like the boxer before he lets loose fury & fire. Its good shes got the anger. Anger can be sharp weapon in the war against yourself.

I demand to know what knowledge you possess of my life, Sir? she goes & Im like The ideas of others steer thy flesh and push thy bone: the needle of thy compass's not thy own.

I am a woman with a sense of freedom, Sir she goes & Im like Nay! Thou thinkest thankest thunkest thou art free but thou art set on roads more fixed than Nuncle carbuncle.

The only roads I am fixed on, Mister Fool are the ones you have fashioned in this spell, this bewitching or whatever Pandora's Box you have contrived to frame on this wretched moor.

Thy true needle is shifted by the magnetic fields of the heart, not a boncebox filled with other people's ideas of morality.

I thunk she was goanny say something else but she pulled her bottom lip under her top wi her tongue crouched down & stroked Nuncles head for a few raindrops then went Will he recover, do you think? & I goes I see, in Nuncle's face, as in a map, the edge of one world and the beginning of another.

We listened to his breath as the rain ticked out the scattered seconds of time on leaves & grass & branches.

You may have spoken to the point, Mister Fool Jane eventually said.

Speak to the end of my shoes? I goes To these bells?

Regarding my moral compass she goes & I let Nuncles breathing answer & eventually she went Yes, yes, on inspection I did forsake love.

She bows her head & goes I am afraid I have quite a low opinion of myself & when I place my hand on hers her arm twitches but her hand stays where it is. I look in her eyes & see beyond her Fool. Shes in turn reflected on the curves of my jellies & her chest heaves when she catches a fleeting glimpse of something shining in her core. Its the woman she will become. Its Jane Eyre.

Could you be honest with me Mister Fool she goes If I were to ask you a direct question?

As honest as any lying Fool. Aye.

How is it that you have come to gather these facts regarding my life?

That I cannot truly say for Foorules forbid me and I cannot say to thee what Foolrule rules may be.

Yet you could relate to me facts from my life?

Didst thou not see Jane? I can tell thee but it pains me, sears me, wriggles me to agony.

You told Nuncle well enough.

Until you could hear. Then the sizzle found me.

The *sizzle* found you?

I reminded her how I was sizzled when I told her name to her & went I could say things but I will sizzle & theres no telling how high the pain nor how long.

Jane thinks & goes Very well Sir. I would not have another being suffer because of me.

There was something about Jane in that moment that made me want to help her.

Thy morality bars thee again I goes & blurt out Bertha is dead!

SIZZLE

The house burnt to the ground!

SIZZLE

Stop Mister Fool!
Rochester is alive!

SIZZLE

Stop Mister Fool. Please stop!

By then Im screaming in agony & sizzled steam rises from the puddle & she goes Shht! Shht! Be silent, Mister Fool & when Im silent she goes But I must say that my heart is thrilled and mind astonished from what you have said, to your detriment, about Rochester being alive! Do not answer she goes & strokes my hair

Aye but many think he'd be better dead.

SIZZLE

Argh!

Why? How? Sorry I should provoke you to speech. You should not answer. Know thee Jane that a woman as low as a toad could love a blind cripple I goes &

SIZZLE

Argh. Argh! They have Lavafied my veins with molten diamonds.

Rochester blind and a cripple? I must find out what is become of him. Are you aware of his current residence? Do not answer that!

I didnt have a fuckin clue even why I was saying this stuff. Foolrules have me say things then punish me. Sick fucks that they are. Fools have in the past been sizzled to lumps of charred wood. You have seen them lying in woods or side-streets & thought them only wood. Some have been not yet dead but creaking as they walk, their mouths a black charcoal hole trying to say salvation, stumbling blind exuding smoke and the pong of death. Every Fool suffers for favours.

Im still writhing in the puddle when Jane suddenly stands & goes If Rochester is alive then I must leave you, Sir, to go to him. I apologise for any pain I have caused thee and thy master. Goodbye she goes & walks off.

But Nuncle wakes abruptly grabs her ankle & goes Where Cordelia?

Let me go, Sir.

Where Cordelia?

We are returned to the heath, Sir goes Jane Where we met. Look, great moors stretch out all around.

Nuncle looks at his free hand & goes Where is Cordelia's body?

Jane crouches down & theres a tone of empathy when she goes Agitation, uncertainty, and an all-predominating confusion scatters my faculties also, Sir, but I truly must leave here now for I have become acutely aware that my salvation lies elsewhere.

Cordelia lives Nuncle goes I feel in my marrow that Cordelia lives & Janes like We witnessed Cordelia die in your arms.

But if time bends, as bend it must have indeed, to bring us back to this blasted heath is it not possible Cordelia lives?

If time truly bends, Sir, all manner of strange things may be possible. Now could you let go of my ankle please she goes.

Cordelia is alive I say. Time has us back. Look see, this raindrop is the one I saw afore. It reflects the same.

Sir goes Jane Objects can occupy the same space at different times or the same times at different spaces. The raindrop is a different raindrop.

Nay, nay, Nuncle goes & hes lost for a moment then a sudden idea hits him & he scans the ground & goes Where be thy line of pebbles, Pignut? & she looks & you can see it dawning on her & Nuncle goes We are in the same space at the same time. Thy disappeared pebbles tell me so.

Release me, Sir, at once!

I tell thee Cordelia lives Nuncle goes & holds tighter wi a grip of joy& shouts Where be my Fool? God a mercy! Boy! Cordelia is not dead! Where be Kent? I mean Caius goes Nuncle & winks at Jane.

Release me from your clutch Sir.

Release thee? Nay! I shall embrace thee Pignut he goes For methinks Time and Space hath knotted in our favour and thou art the cause.

He wraps himself around Janes legs & shes a plank of Victorian mahogany as Nuncle climbs her body hugs her tight & goes Sweets with sweets war not, joy delights in joy! She's not dead! Cordelia not dead! Ye Gods speed me to my Daughter. I must see proof of this & he goes I summons Good Caius winking at Jane again Listen well he goes & shouts No, I will be the pattern of all patience; I will say nothing.

Lightning cracks a sheet of nuclear white. Nuncles drive to see Cordelia has us accelerating through the *play*.

Thunder headpresses earthumps & when we raise our heads Kent is coming through the storm.

ACT III SCENE II. Another part of the heath. Storm ftill. Enter Kent

Kent goes to a dripping shivering Nuncle Alas, Sir, are you here? Things that love night love not such nights as these; the wrathful skies gallow the very wanderers of the dark.

ACT III SCENE IV. The
heath. Before a hovel

Poor Toms a cold! Poor Tom's a cold!

Come to shelter your grace.

Tom eye bulges, Gloucester observes. Caius fiddles. Jane notes.

Nuncle goes Come, good Athenian.

ACT III SCENE VI. A chamber in a farmhoufe adjoining the caftle.

Bring in the evidence goes Nuncle & I hold up one sheeps head.

Thou robed man of justice, take thy place.

Goneril on a shovel Regan on a rake.

ACT IV SCENE VI. Fieldſ near Do ver. Enter KING LEAR, fantaſti cally dreſſed with wild flowerſ

If you're going to San Francisco be sure to wear some flowers in your hair.

Jane makes her way toward Nuncle.

ACT IV SCENE VII. A tent in the French camp. LEAR on a bed afleep

Heres Cordelia wi her sword on Janes neck. Nuncles being attended by a Doctor who goes Madam, do you 'tis fittest & Cordelia overleans Nuncle & goes How does my royal Lord? How fares your Majesty?

Nuncle brainforms Cordeila & goes You have been taken out o' the grave. My soul is in bliss; these tears are like sunshine.

Sir, do you know me? goes Cordelia & Nuncle sits up wi his palms on the grass blinks blinks again & goes You are my daughter Cordelia. You did not die. Begad she did not die. She lives! She died once and lives again! Tis true! Oh Joy.

He is still, still, far wide! goes Cordelia.

Where hast thou been? goes Nuncle Oh daylight so fair! I have another chance.

O, look upon me, Sir, and hold your hands in benediction o'er me goes Cordelia & Nuncle goes I am in perfect mind &

wraps himself around her legs like he done wi Jane & Cordelias like No, Sir, you must not but Nuncle upreaches going Be
your tears wet? Yes, 'faith. I pray, weep not. If you have poison
for me, I would drink it for love of thee.

My King shall drink to victory's sweet breath goes Cordelia & helps him up going Will't please your Highness walk?

Nuncle struggles up & wi a smile for a miraculous day he
limps off wi Cordelia. His voice is soft as he goes You must
bear with me. I am filled with joy. I have been foolish but now
old, now wise. Listen to your father dear Cordelia. I will tell a
truth to thee...

Bzzz bzzz & all is suddenly dark. Then
were rolling through clouds.

ACT V SCENE II. A field be
tween the two campſ.

Alarum within. Enter, with drum and colourſ, KING LEAR, CORDE
LIA, and Soldierſ, over the ſtage; and exeunt

Nuncle Cordelia & the French army march to war.

Lightning.   Thunder.

ACT V SCENE III. The Brit
iſh camp near Dover.

Enter, in conqueſt, with drum and colourſ, EDMUND, KING LEAR
and CORDELIA, priſonerſ; Captain, Soldierſ, & c

Where art thou Cordelia?
She's gone, Sir.
Away?
Yes Sir.

ACT V SCENE III. The Britifh camp
near Dover. Reenter KING LEAR,
with CORDELIA dead in hif armf

Cordelias hair moves in the breeze. Nuncles head drops

down.

returned to the heath (2)

Im spat into the gorse bushes & pulling fuckin thorns from my shins when I hear Nuncle let out a quiet Cordelia! He inspects his hands & goes Cordelia?

She lived again and died again Nuncle.

Nuncle goes Help me Pignut. Thou must help me. I tried to advise my daughter but she was headstrong for war and had me mad when I suggesteth otherwise. She ran us down different roads to the same destination.

But Jane goes Sir, I do not know what *this* is but it seems some kind of unchangeable, immutable destiny is written in *this*. And if destiny has Cordelia die then I fear it may not be changed. However, Sirs she goes nodding to Nuncle & me As I have only stumbled into *this* then I feel it is morally appropriate of me to stumble out.

Nay! Nay! Thou art of help to the King.

I am afraid, Sirs, from your presence I must go.

But my Cordelia! My hope of heaven!

You must seek your hope without my assistance, for I too

must seek my one chance of heaven, my one hope of the true, eternal Paradise. Goodbye and good luck she goes takes a sharp turn & is gone.

Off she pops madness and frocks Nuncle I goes & when her footsteps are indistinguishable from the storm Nuncle goes Our quest is utterly bereft Fool; all is lost & he flops to the ground sobbing.

& at this point I have to accept hes right. I prepare myself for eternity on the heath & start dragging boughs & branches together to make some kinda shelter.

But oft luck hits where hope is coldest. Im dragging a large straight log through the gorse when theres this rustling & outpops Jane shaking rain from her head. Her eyes pop & her shoulders drop & I go There's no escaping thy fate & shes like I have been walking hour upon hour. Perhaps even days without dawn. Out there. I struck straight into the heath; I held on to a hollow I saw deeply furrowing the brown moorside; I waded knee-deep in its dark growth; I turned with its turnings, and finding a moss-blackened granite crag in a hidden angle, I sat down under it. High banks of moor were about me but when I moved I came again to this place.

Nuncle goes The Gods have us trapped. Yet there was a time, Pignut, before thee arrived when fate had for us straight plans not circular.

& I went Aye Jane! Thou dis-proportionate us in every part, like to a chaos, or an unlick'd bear-whelp.

Ha she goes her anger seeping out Mister Fool, I never dreamt I would be entrapped into an absurd union with a defrauded wretch, badly bound to a bad, mad, and embruted tyrant! But it seems I am and therefore I must question what sort of human being I have been to deserve such a purgatory as this.

Nuncle is no Brute you flying excuse for a skeleton I goes Nuncle listen not.

But Nuncle isnt listening anyhow. His boncebox is chasing a fading white dream of Cordelia. His last disappearing mote of salvation.

Fixed nay Nuncle goes slowly We are not locked like the fixed stars of heaven. Fixed nay. We can fly to Dover nay? To Cordelia? No, I will be the pattern of all... goes Nuncle but Jane clamps her hand over his gub & his words muffle out indistinguishable from the wind & ineffective. Nothing happens except a wee tree shudder & a spark like a torch wi a dud battery petering out soon as you switch it on.

Nuncles like She hath the King spit his words into her palm! & I go Like thee the wind and rain Jane? I go.

Pardon?

If Nuncle says not these words we shall bedfellow eternity kissing this storm.

And what then if he does, Mister Fool? she goes For twice we have relived his tragedy and arrived back to this wretched place from which we cannot leave!

Here we are and here we be it seems its here for ye and me I go & plant my arse on a wet rock wave my arms at the sky & go This is a fair roofless house. Dost thou think the rain shall stop any time?

Sirs, Mister Lear and Mister Fool, for some logic defying reason that very sentence catapults us through the play, the story, the whatever it is. Through Time!

And Space I go & Nuncles like What the Gods know, we know only part. Those words shall abort Cordelia's death, or I die by attempting goes Nuncle pointing where he thinks Cordelia might be & going No, I will be the pattern…

But Jane clamps him again & goes If I may… before you do utter these words again, could we perhaps take some time to calculate the possibility of changing your or my relative positions?

Nuncle goes Old men, fools and children calculate, so the old saying goes & Jane wi determination scribbled on her face goes Mister Fool chance has meted you a measure of intelligence exceeding that which you have chosen to display: that I know. So may I suggest we rally our collective wits and instigate some strange expedient to achieve escape from this oppressive moor.

Ha! I go Thou hast tried to go there or where and came back here thinking here was there & now thee are here wanting to go there again. Thou art not all there.

She stares into the storm for a while then goes It is clear then, Mister Fool, that if we can't change things here on this moor, if they are in fact immutable, then we have no choice but to change things there. In *The Tragedy Of King Lear.*

I fling my wet palm out Spiderman style in agreement nod my jingle bell & she goes Will you help me Mister Fool? Will you help your master?

I paused cos the way she asked for help was kinda kinda well sweet like. There was truly another side to plain loaf Jane & it was coming out as Foolrules predicted. I was beginning to like this assignment. So I goes Nuncle listen with thy lugs, thy foolish self, thy Fool & Nutpigs should now draw our Bonceboxes together in mutual conference & fashion deep plots of what needs change for this Tragedy to end.

Approach, to confer about these matters Nuncle goes What says ye Pignut?

But there's an uneasiness about Nuncle. Hes like a man signing on for Jobseekers when theres a warrant out for his arrest.

We must make a list Mister Lear goes Jane & Nuncles like List? I list to the moon. Plead to the storm.

A list of possible scenarios Jane goes.

Shalt I speak the line Nuncle goes & Janes like You must wait till you are called to act.

Nuncles old arrogance rises up to that slight an he goes I will not wait pinion'd at your court. Nor once be chastised with the sober eye of dull Pignut.

Mister Lear...! Jane goes but Nuncle raises his hands & goes Lo, ere I can repeat this curse again even for so short a space in sweet Cordelia's company & he goes No, I will be the pattern of all patience; I will say nothing.

shaka lack! Thrice we tumble

through the play.

1   Whoſ there? ſhoutſ Caiuſ. Poor Tomſ a cold! Poor Tomſ a cold! Bring in the evidence. If youre going to San Francifco be fure to wear fome flowerf in your hair. How doeſ my royal Lord? Nuncle holdſ Cordeliaſ legſ. Cordelia & heir army march to war. Wherefore art thou Cordelia? Cordelia ſwingſ from a black hazel.

2   Whoſ there? ſhoutſ Caiuſ. Poor Tomſ a cold! Poor Tomſ a cold! Bring in the evidence. If youre going to San Francifco be fure to wear fome flowerf in your hair. How doeſ my royal Lord? Nuncle holdſ Cordeliaſ legſ. Cordelia & heir army march to war. Wherefore art thou Cordelia? Cordelia ſwingſ from a black hazel.

3   Whoſ there? ſhoutſ Caiuſ. Poor Tomſ a cold! Poor Tomſ a cold! Bring in the evidence. If youre going to San Francifco be fure to wear fome flowerf in your hair. How doeſ my royal Lord? Nuncle holdſ Cordeliaſ legſ. Cordelia & heir army march

to war. Wherefore art thou Cordelia? Cordelia ſwingſ from a
black hazel.

returned to the heath (5)

Nuncles exhausted fatigued shattered & beat & I feel like a crisp poke shrivelling up at a bonfire. Nuncle knows by now the Cordelia he holds in his arms each time is but a ghost. He stretches his lips wide in grief & hobbles into the bush. I can hear grunting & sobbing & me & Pignut exchange worryfull glances till he returns wi the doe by the ears. Its a horrific sight this dug up hare. Its eyes pop death into the maw of the storm & its tongue purple wi the stiffening cold of death sticks out to the left like a clowns.

Nuncle holds her to the sky & goes She is truly dead. Truly and completely dead. In memory of her when her ashes, in an urn more precious than the rich-jewel'd coffer of Darius, transported shall be at high festivals before the Kings and Queens of France.

His shoulders shudder like a pneumatic drill as he holds the Doe close to his chest & goes Cordelia. My Sweet Cordelia.

Jane takes the Doe gently from his hands & goes I shall take care of her my Lord & she makes a face I kinda understand. An acknowledgement that the Doe is a lightning rod to the true nature of his grief. Jane goes into the bush to re-bury the Doe. The robin in a flurry of rainwater follows.

Nuncle crouches sobbing into his hands & Im thinking hes finally lost the plot when he upspeaks like a sane man.

Fool, lend me your ears. Sit and lend me thy ears, Boy. I am ready. I am ready to put armour on for though my soul disputes well with my sense, that this may be some error, but no madness, yet doth this accident and flood of misfortune so far exceed all instance, all discourse, that I am ready to distrust mine eyes and wrangle with my reason, that persuades me to any other trust but that I am mad, or else Pignut's mad.

& at that Pignut arrives back wi dirt in her fingernails & tears in her eyes & goes If Pignut, as is your want to call me Sir, were insane, hers is a very cool and collected insanity. But I am not mad, Sir, and perhaps in this strange place where fiction, fact, space and time are entwined, neither are you nor Mister Fool.

Shall we on without apology? goes Nuncle but the tilt of her head says she wants one & she goes Could you agree, Sir, to desist, from speaking *that* line?

I serve you apology goes Nuncle You have my very silence and my patience. Proceed, proceed: we will begin these rites.

Jane looks at Nuncle deciding if hes serious then goes Sir, there are decisions made in each of our lives which, if one had power to undo then the course of one's life may be steered away from tragedy & Nuncle goes Speak ye of points whereon a mote did turn the balance? & shes like Yes. Yes. Exactly. A step, a look or gesture, a tiny word or decision, perhaps blank of meaning at the time of making but, in reality, disastrous.

And thou hast made these decisions? goes Nuncle & Janes like Of course I have. We have all made them Sir. Decision. De scission, to scissor, to cut one path off in favour of another, finally and completely she goes & I goes You mumbled before, your mumbleness, to have plans for Nuncle & shes like Yes, the moments in the plot, your life, or whatever *this* is, the play, the moments when, for the want of a wiser decision and against the advice of fairer men, you provoke Divine justice to pursue its course and disasters come thick on you.

My mind pushes 'gainst the shoulder of my sail? goes Nuncle & Janes like Yes Sir, yes! Eloquently put, one's mind is the compass of one's life & Nuncle goes Mmm & backruns recent events like a Netflix rewind. I see it all stepping past inside his eyebubbles. The eyes are the windows of the bowl – of porridge.

I watch Nuncle consider every crossroad node point & junction in the satnav of his life. Regretting. Re-calculating. He upstraights & goes Oh to have the spell to undo these knots of harm. We might touch sourest points with sweetest terms.

He armreaches Jane & goes I am ready to put armour on. Pignut may advise the King.

Thank you Sir Jane goes I shall continue. For instance, if you recall when Mister Fool advised you retreat to shelter, you could have gone back to your daughters'. May I ask why not?

The Pelicans? Never! armfolds Nuncle & Jane goes And there it is plainly.

Speak your opinions Nuncle goes & Janes like If I may say so Sir, your attitude, that very attitude you have just displayed, leads you to make decisions which, stacked upon each other, day after day, build a tragedy.

Put but a little water in the spoon, Pignut I goes.

This is no time for soft ministry, Mister Fool.

Nuncle goes Thy medicine would be I change a thousand, a million decisions, already sent to chaos the world? I must dis-knot the fisherman's net?

No Sir, for each knot in that net is tied to another ad infinitum.

What linsey-woolsey hast thou to speak Pignut Nuncle goes & shes like If I were in your place and could untie only one single knot, I would choose that hour you divided your kingdom.

One knot undone can free a kingdom?

I am hoping against logic and natural reason that one knot, should we find a way to undo it, can untie the whole tangled tragedy.

Nuncle stands in silence rain dripping from his hands like long fluid silver fingernails.

In that one moment, Jane goes Sir, had you but listened to Cordelia, you could have changed the course of history.

Nuncle goes I did list her. I list her and heard only nothings monster'd.

Sir, Cordelia tried to warn you of her sisters' deceptions.

In honestest defence. I heard her not, Pignut.

Nevertheless she did attempt to warn you Sir.

Why did I hear not, Fool?

I know not Nuncle. Have I thy children's voices? Thy monstrous lugs?

You did not hear, Sir, because she spoke in asides goes Jane & Im like Ha! Rats with donkey's ears cannot hear asides & Nuncle quickspeaks Nay, nay, it is worth the listening Fool. For Pignut canst hear asides.

You are too much mistaken in this Nuncle I goes & hes like Pignut can hear asides I tell thee. She heard my asides anon. Mine eyes and ears do her whispers witness.

Nay!

Yeah!

Anon?

Anon boy. To the last breathed syllable of sound.

A witch then stands before us, Nuncle.

Nay! Let witchcraft be for now he goes Ask her, see what her lips say.

28

pignut doth hear afidef!

Thou canst hear asides, Pignut? I goes Yes of course I can she says like Id asked if she could breathe & even though I fine well knew she could hear asides Foolrules have me aside to Nuncle We shall put this skinny witch to examination Nuncle & he agreenods.

Jane eyerolls sighs & goes Examine me if it be your wish, Mister Fool & I go for the full on hunner percent aside into the mouth of the storm I go May not an ass know when the cart draws the horse? Whoop, Jug! then go What did I spake runt? & she pendulums her head as she monotones May not & ass know when the cart draws the horse? Whoop. Jug.

Argh! I go for effect Zounds! Nuncle she hears asides!

Examine further that thine eyes might see truth boy Nuncle goes & I ahems aphlegms spits & goes Thin and bloodless lips and pancake tits & Nuncle, forgetting his troubles giggles rain dripping from top to bottom lip like a laughcage. Jane not best pleased has a wee fly look at her pancakes & contemptifeyes me.

119

Again goes Nuncle Aside again boy. See thee that she hath in truth the gift.

You try old fool and we'll double see her witchyness.

I try?

Yes Nuncle you speak. I will watch her peepers do not wander thy lips, turn thee away Pignut.

She turns away & folds her arms. Nuncle winks inbreathes & asides Darkness and devils! Saddle my horses; call my train together: Degenerate bastard! I'll not trouble thee. Yet have I left a daughter then he turns & goes I have finished & Im like Well? Of what did he spake J anus? & she goes Darkness and devils! Saddle my horses; call my... train something: Degenerate I won't say that word! I'll not trouble thee. Something something something left a daughter.

Tis proved goes Nuncle & Im like She hears but what strange matter is this? She can hear asides Nuncle? Tis just as rare as virgin brides but Nuncle has moodswung down & he goes to Jane What then prithee good woman were Cordelia's asides?

Do you remember, Sir, when Goneril professed her love... that she loved you more than words can wield the matter?

Dearer than eye-sight, goes Nuncle Space, and liberty. Pah! Pah! Pah! Beyond what can be valued, Pah! Pah! Pah! rich or rare. Clump mouthed Pelican!

And tosses thee to the storm like a flea ridden hound Nuncle! I go but Jane patches me & goes When Goneril had finished speaking Sir, Cordelia then spoke an aside.

How now? Spake Cordelia how? Her plausive words?

She said What shall Cordelia do? Love, and be silent goes Jane & Nuncles like a fragile statue overchipped by the sculptors pins before he quietly goes Oh! The sea enraged is not half so deaf as a foolish King. Speak again.

What shall Cordelia do? Love, and be silent goes Pignut.

I swear to thee, Pignut, by the white hand of Cordelia, I heard it not. Fool was it in thine ears?

No Nuncle, I heard only thy reply to Goneril.

The devil our ears took captive? Come on my boy, for this ear is deaf, speak! Thoust must have heard some?

Nay I did not Nuncle for twould be the end of the world if man and filly did hear asides for we would know each other's thoughts. Twould be the war to end all wars.

Cordelia's next aside? Nuncle goes & Pignuts like After Regan professed that she found no joy in life except in her love for you, Cordelia asided thus, Then poor Cordelia! And yet not so; since, I am sure, my love's more richer than my tongue.

More richer than my tongue Nuncle goes & deep in I see faint hope flicker. Like someone trying to spark a lighter in a cold & windy Glasgow bus stop. Nuncle goes Again, please I beseech thee! & Pignuts like Then poor Cordelia! And yet not so; since, I am sure, my love's more richer than my tongue.

Nuncle stumbles.

I get him by the tricep & go How now my Lord? & hes like Eh? & I go Dost thou see a ghost? & hes like A ghost riding the bounds of my heart & Pignuts like The plain facts are, Sir, that Cordelia loves you and your two devious and avaricious daughters do not.

Nuncle mutters Forests and rivers and wide-skirted meads! Then he says it to a sudden patch of stars All for forests and rivers and wide-skirted meads fate deals me death!

The doors of grief are blasted open. Nuncle ingulps like an asthma attack till he can speak. He goes I have chosen the pink glow of pride over the pale complexion of love.

Pride and power can blind a man to truth goes Pignut & Nuncle murmurs She loved me, she loved me, she loved me. My great decision hath much blood let forth. Apollo take me back to my first course. Oh Fool what is a king to do?

I open my mouth & squeak but Pignut goes Say those words again if you will, Sir & hes like Words? I have had words to my gizzard. If life be words then I die to silence.

Please, Sir, trust me. Could you say those words again? & he delivers them deadpan Let Mars divide eternity in twain, set a huge mountain 'tween my heart and tongue. My great decision hath much blood let forth. Apollo take me back to my first course.

Perfect goes Pignut Utterly perfect.

Tis?

I think that we may have a solution of the enigma that perplexes us.

We have only been worse confounded in our attempts to leave this bog, Pignut I goes and we are cast back instanter following a five hour shit trudge & shes like Yes. Yes. Exactly & Im like Bang your boncebox for it has stopped turning & she goes We tried to leave physically, to walk away from fate.

But fate has out-manoeuvred us every time.

Yeah goes I none the wiser.

Don't you see Mister Fool?

As a bat in sunlight. Thy point is blunt as a Frenchman's head.

Spit thee words as apple seeds goes Nuncle Cans't thy magic bear us to that fated day Pignut? Nuncle goes wi the wild eyes of a child & Pignut goes There seems to be some impulse or force which we don't understand. It seems, and this day has proved it, that we are blind to the true nature of things, so perhaps, Sir, if you were to utter, with great conviction, the lines which precede the division of the kingdom then...

The idea crosses Nuncles face like a sweep of sunlight & he goes Where time has not scythed all that I began! & shes like Yes. Yes, Sir, and on this occasion thwarting the urge to banish Cordelia, you grant her one third of your kingdom & Nuncles like I'll follow thee, I'll follow thee Pignut and make a heaven of hell. How shall this purpose shine?

Pignut goes Can you remember the lines Sir? & Nuncles like Yeah. Yeah. I entered the hall. I entered the hall and... I have the words in my head shalt I roll them from my tongue?

Pignut checks wi me I nod & she goes Yes. Yes, Sir & Nuncle closes his eyes builds up an energy looks like hes having a shit in fact & goes Attend the lords of France and Burgundy, Gloucester.

He listens to the rain & wind then opens his eyes one at a time & goes louder Attend the lords of France and Burgundy,

Gloucester.

But theres no change.

Attend the lords of France and Burgundy, Gloucester!

Pignut goes Try Meantime we shall express our darker purpose & Nuncle takes a breath & bellows Meantime we shall express our darker purpose and…

Nothing happens.

Nuncle tries again as if louder does a better job. Nothing. Only the persistent hiss of the rain & its chaotic drumming on the leaves & the gusts of wind straining the tree & a plummeting sense of disappointment.

There is no going back in time I goes Tis impossible & Pignuts like Oh yes there is Mister Fool for have we not just come back to this time from a battle in the future? & I scratch my coconut at her rightness.

So why the Gods allow us back down the laces of time only to this knot and no further goes Nuncle & we three thunk until Nuncle points at Pignut & goes Thee! & shes like Me?

Aye. Thee. Thou sayest thou comest from the future year eighteen and twenty eight.

I did say it, Sir, for that is the truth.

Then in some witchcraft thy future, if it be truth, hath crashed against my presence on the heath. As I screamed Hurricanoes etcetera etcetera thy arrival opened future loops and did drop a veil betwixt today and all our yesterdays which we cannot penetrate.

It made a crazy sense that two causes instead of causing

two effects merge & cause one effect much greater than the sum of the parts. Like two trains running in the same direction converging in a tunnel & instead of exploding they physically merge but the tunnel collapses as they leave. They can go more powerfully to all stations beyond but never back through that tunnel again.

In other words were fucked.

What are thy thoughts Fool goes Nuncle & Im like It's like two horses, Nuncle, running in the same direction, converging in a tunnel and instead of injury they merge together blood and bone, becoming a monstrous eight legged two headed beast whilst the tunnel collapses behind them. They can ride to all points beyond but never back through that tunnel again.

Except, Mister Fool, we can't go to all points goes Pignut We can only go to predestined points. All the scenes King Lear appears in. No more.

My metaphor must change then, Pignut I go So the eight legged two headed monstrous horse, when it jumps a hedge, it jumps a thousand fields. Will that quench thy metathirst?

There is no going back from this moor, Sirs, under whichever current metaphors, laws of science, or realities we are operating under. Therefore we must go forward from here but, this time however, with a logical plan.

O Isis! 'tis possible?

While there is breath there must be hope goes Pignut & Nuncle goes Joy and all comfort to thy breast Pignut if thou canst save my daughter's soul!

A tear on Nuncles cheek wobbles different from the rain.

Like a jelly. Like its alive then drops into another universe to seek out Cordelia. Like were in the Phenomenal universe and Cordelias in the Noumenal that Nuncle Immanuel used to bump his philosophical gums about.

What says thee to this Fool? Eh? Nuncle goes & Im like If Nuncle could save his daughter's life I would vomit with joy!

I pray he goes Awake, Pignut: if you love Cordelia, bend thoughts and wits to achieve her & Pignuts like I am willing to aid you to the utmost of my power in a purpose so honest, Sir.

She fingerwiggles ideas into her head flinging them out again till she finds one she likes.

We could persuade Caius, Kent, when he arrives, after you, Sir, utter that line, to speed to Dover and warn Cordelia. Send a message to abort the attack.

Nay! Nay goes Nuncle For then the Pelican sisters rule repugnant!

Yes Sir, but Cordelia does not die. She lives and you live. To perhaps fight another day?

Nuncle nods in answer to his own questions. A rivulet of rain streams from his bobbing nose then he goes Tis a great design. My good Kent, my loyal Kent, a goodman. I have twice mistaken good for treachery and I am today's fool for that. Poor Kent goes in disguise and penury for the love of his King. Now must his conscience my acquaintance seal.

No Sir goes Pignut No. You must act as a King unaware Caius is Kent & Nuncles like Further injure my good companion? & Pignut goes We cannot risk upsetting these fragile balances to unpredictable effect as you have witnessed yourself already, Sir.

I see the bottom of your purpose. Disturb not the tapestry of the stars goes Nuncle Thy mind works outside the easy roads Pignut! Shalt the King utter his line?

Yes Sir goes Pignut & we duck down for the thunder & lightning & Nuncle mutters into his tunic No, I will be the pattern of all patience; I will say nothing.

Lightning.   ing Thunder.

29

ACT III SCENE II. Another part of the heath. Storm ftill. Enter Kent

Kent shouts Who's there? & Im like automatic Marry, here's grace and a cod-piece; that's a wise man and a Fool & Kent goes to a shivering Nuncle Alas, Sir, are you here? Things that love night love not such nights as these; the wrathful skies gallow the very wanderers of the dark.

Nuncle asides I am sore of heart. I should not have banished this good man. Pignut hears it & I pretend I don't.

Kent waits for Nuncle to speak but Nuncles lost in guilt so Pignut goes Caius, Sir, the King requests you ride with haste to Dover where you should instruct Cordelia to abort the French invasion.

But Kents eyes stay on Nuncle so Pignut whispers I know you are Kent & he eyebulges & asides She knows I am Kent how come this witchery? & Pignuts like It is not witchery Mister Caius & Kent asides Gadzooks! She hears my asides!

Yes Sir, I do.

He ignores Pignut & tries to stare some words out of Nuncle but Pignut goes I ask you again, Sir, will you ride to Dover and warn Cordelia to abort her war. Catastrophe awaits her.

Kent doesnt even move his eyes. He stares at Nuncle all robot like & when he realises Nuncles not goanny speak he goes Alack, bare-headed! Gracious my Lord, hard by here is a hovel. Some friendship will it lend you 'gainst the tempest.

I prefer the rain good stranger goes Nuncle placing his hand on Kents shoulder & Kents like Then if my Lord prefer the rain your loyal subject sire will love the rain aside him.

Nay, nay good Caius, I have here my protectors.

My Lord, I shall be thy shelter until rescue removes you from this heath Kent goes & Nuncle softens & goes Thou remindest me of my good servant Kent whom I wrongly banished & Pignut pokes a sharp elbow under Nuncles ribs. He expels a wee offt & Kent takes a tiny backstep gathers his sensicles & goes I know not this fellow Kent of whom ye speak sire but Pignut whispers again about riding to Dover & Kent hisses I shalt stay with my Lord & Nuncles like Pignut doth whisper thee?

This woman just this moment hath whispered me, aye my Lord.

And what prithee doth she whisper?

I should be silent and not speak, my Lord.

Good and loyal Caius, I command thou speak it.

My Lord, methinks she is mad as a donkeys nose in thorns.

Thou hast my blessing as thy King to speak out her whispers goes Nuncle & Kent goes This woman whispered me ride to Dover Sir and request Cordelia abort the invasion.

Kent shrinks into himself expecting Nuncles rage but Nuncle goes My good Caius thou shouldst listen to this witch's whispering for therein speaks an awful truth.

But why make speed to Dover my Lord? Are ye in possession of informations? Dost thou have other designs to pour war into the bowels of your ungrateful daughters?

Knowest thou of my Pelican daughters?

Yeah my Lord for the land is alive with its injustice. I say again my Lord, dost thou have designs to pour war on your ungrateful daughters?

Nay goes Nuncle Nay. We seek peace & Kents like Ye seek peace when your kingdom is in ruins? Britain be fortunate and flourish in peace and plenty 'tis still a dream, or else such stuff as madmen.

Good Caius, there are plans afoot of which the King cannot speak. Thou must attend his majesty's command.

If I be bold enough your grace, I would be protector of his excellence.

Nay! Nay! Fly to Dover.

I stay with my Lord and the storm till rescue brings its succour or we die out here of cold.

Kent takes a soldiers stance & exasperated Nuncle looks at me & I looks at Pignut & we thrice shake heads & Pignut goes Perhaps we should relate to good Caius what the future holds & up pricks Caiuss ears. Nuncle goes Proceed. Reveal to this man thy powers, Pignut. List to the witch good Caius.

Pignut goes Caius, you have just sent a man to Cordelia with a message about how the King is being treated by his daughters & Kents head whipsstares her feet to head to toe to eyes & she goes How could I possibly know this, Sir?

A messenger passing through the storm with tales and informations could have whispered thee.

Nuncle nods for Pignut to go on. She wipes rain from her lips & goes You have scribbled a note warning Cordelia that there is division between Albany and Cornwall and that the French have men on the ground ready to join forces against them.

Tales and informations! goes Caius & Pignuts like I could repeat your exact words yet only you and this one other man were present.

Speak me then this intelligence, if thou hast a witchcraft.

You said, Sir, If you shall see Cordelia, as fear not but you shall, show her this ring and she will tell you who your fellow is.

Kent chews the inside of his cheek. Nuncle steps forward & goes That letter ye must steal away bravely, and more good Caius, more, ye must warn Cordelia to retreat. To flee to France.

And into certain destruction cast the King? Nay!

If thou trust me good Caius, if thou trust me as I trust thee, and tis sure I do trust thee, then tis all for the kingdom's good for there are dark portents.

Kent looks at Nuncle thinks for a second & goes Good my Lord. I shall act thy wish but I have my own humble conditions.

Nuncle nods & goes Speak these humble conditions good Caius and, if pleasing to thy King, he shall be bound with an oath to yield.

As my love for my King cannot be made greater, I wish for his wellbeing and so, Lord, I beg of thee to retreat to the Hovel I have described. Then I shalt ride on clouds of content to the place where good Cordelia lies and warn of these portents.

Nuncle smiles like a plastic clown pulls off one of Caiuss gloves clasps his hand & bids him Gods swiftest wings of speed. Caius points in the direction of the hovel & promises to bring Cordelia to tryst with her father there.

Good morrow good Caius goes Nuncle & Kent disappears into the swirling cloud & I go Wait a while Nuncle lest the fool ends up back here.

He doth make sense, Pignut Nuncle goes Better plot and plan under a roof with a fire.

When theres no sense of his return I go Hes not caught up in the swirls of this place like us Nuncle & Pignut goes Let us see if our plan works & Nuncle takes a breath & goes My good boy. Come, bring us to this hovel.

Lightning flashes. Thunder s.

30

ACT III SCENE IV. The
heath. Before a hovel

The dilapidated wooden door creaks like a crushed rat.

Good my Lord, enter here I goes & Nuncles like Prithee, go in thyself & Im like I'll go in first after you go in first Nuncle & I go in dustdragging my damp shoe bells.

Fathom and half, fathom and half! says Poor Tom! & I go Tom Tom Bedlam we have your King here and a woman.

Wanderers, Poor Tom hath news for thee from Dover

Dover? Thou hast news from Dover? goes Nuncle & Poor Toms like Aye! Thou shalt not defy the foul fiend who still through the hawthorn blows the cold wind: Says suum, mun, ha, no, nonny. Dolphin my boy, my boy, sessa! let him trot by.

Poor Tom dances around the hovel & Nuncle tries to set him down the right road by going Why, thou wert better in thy grave than to answer with thy uncovered body this extremity of the skies. Is man no more than this? Off, off, you lendings! Come unbutton here.

I go Prithee, Nuncle, be contented; 'tis a naughty night to swim in. Look, here comes a walking fire.

We peer into the night for that thin light that should come a wandering toward our hovel but nothing comes & Nuncles like Wherefore Gloucester? & Poor Tom goes. Gloucester is dead my Lord.

Dead? Good Gloucester? Dead?

In the battle at Dover goes Poor Tom.

But there is no battle at Dover goes Pignut & Poor Tom goes Good Caius did ride hard to Cordelia fearing the King woudst die of shivering cold on the stormy heath, with a fool and a lady clown. He bade Cordelia attack immediate and catch the foul sisters a napping.

The battle rages? goes Nuncle.

Nay goes Poor Tom The hurlyburly's done. The battle's lost and won.

And good Cordelia? goes Nuncle.

Cordelia captured by Goneril and Regan, they torture her for pleasure by night and hunt with hounds the King by day. Fie, foh, and fum, I smell the blood of a British King.

& at that theres a great & a great flash unlike before & were fired through chaos to

ACT V SCENE III The Britiſh camp near Dover.

In the aftermath of the battle Cordelia is lashed to a distant pole surrounded by putrefying bodies of mangled French soldiers.

O, horrible! O, horrible! most horrible! goes Nuncle cos Regan & Goneril are taking turns at hacking into Cordelia wi swords.

The swing of the sword.

The wrenching back of Cordelias head.

The thwack of the blade.

Cordelias squeal.

Regan lays one into her thigh. Goneril spins Bruce Lee stylee & fuckyi chops off Cordelias arm just below the shoulder. Regan picks up the arm & knocks Cordelia about the head wi it. Cackling between thumps.

Nuncle stumbleruns over the bodies screaming Butchers and villains! Bloody cannibals! How sweet a plant have you untimely cropp'd!

& when he gets there he wraps himself around Cordelia as protection but the sisters shout Goodmorrow father & lay swords into him. Regan scudding him now & then on the bonce wi the severed arm.

These are his words as they chop You have no children, butchers! If you had, the thought of them would have stirr'd up remorse: but if you ever chance to have a child, look in her youth to have her so cut as, deathwomen, you have rid this sweet young princess!

They hack Nuncle & Cordelia across & up & down to meaty ribbons & leave them to bleed white on the post as a kinda lesson to the power hungry brutes of war & as me & Pignut try to escape to fuck knows where were surrounded & captured.

Pignuts tied to a post to be burnt as a witch. The cunts

nail me to a cross & write **REX STULTI** above it on a bit of wood.

I the distance see Nuncle & Cordelias hacked bodies white as a soap powder advert across the battlefield. The Pelicans set the sticks & straws aflame at Pignuts feet. She screams at them in anger she goes This is not over yet. Right shall prevail over your deeds. But the flames singe her face & her hair catches fire & she screams. Thats when I see Cordelias head fall down then Nuncles. The skies turn black. Lightning strikes my

cross &

returned to the heath (6)

Sput back onto the moor Pignut coughs invisible smoke from her lungs & dances a wee jig on ghostly flames before realising shes free.

Thank you she goes to the stones Whatever you are. You have snatched me from a horrible and excruciating death

Nuncles coconut clears & he goes The wild dog shall flesh his tooth on every innocent. O my poor kingdom, sick with hellish blows!

Once we clear our heads it becomes clear that every time we interfere fate deals out a darker world. Its like Cambodia in the wake of Nuncle Pol Pot out there. The Pelican rotten-dotter sisters are running amok putting the kingdom & all philosophies of order to flame. Regan & Goneril are goanny make the whole world suffer. Acres of bones will fill the fields. Disagreers disembowelled. We speak long & we speak deep but every solution brings wi it the possibility of an afore un-imagined darkness.

Eventually Nuncle stops the conversation & goes Out

there, whether the King is present or no, it seems, armies of pestilence shall strike all children yet unborn and unbegot, where those Pelican daughters reign. Yet on this heath from hour to hour, we ripe and ripe, and then, from hour to hour, we rot and rot. Now, Fool? How like you our choices that you stand pensive, as half malcontent?

Ye present but choices two Nuncle when there may be a million beyond our knowledge I goes knowing that across the mystical walls of the Foolrules lies an energy replete wi chance & choice & everlasting life but the claustrophobic physicality of this phenomenal reality made us (them)(you) effectively blind to it. Or simpler put: the key is on a high shelf.

All things have a cause, Sirs, goes Pignut And an effect. The cause of those most recent and horrible events was Kent riding to Dover and causing Cordelia to attack too early, before her French allies were fully assembled. Perhaps in another scenario, with a well prepared army, Cordelia may be well equipped to annihilate the Pelican Daughters, as you describe them, Sir.

Nuncle goes But our every act sends my good daughter to deaths most terrible. I am sorry for us: by our own acts we art condemn'd.

I have nothing more profitable to suggest then, Sir, than we make certain Kent, when next he arrives, is prevented from riding to Dover and thus, we may lay our plans accordingly, to assist Cordelia to victory.

Next he arrives! When Kent next arrives? Nuncle bellows A next there shalt not be. Should we let loose hell? Boy! Hear thee Pignut's most outrageous fit of madness?

I do Nuncle I says & goes to Pignut I was nailed to a tree like a comedy Jesus. They tried to burn thee, set fire to thy hair & Pignuts like Nonetheless an eternity here, as we have discussed ad infinitum, is worse than a legion of such as we experienced. As you must have noticed, Sirs, no matter how ghastly and horrible that experience, we are catapulted back to this place and this time. Perhaps we were made to suffer and our suffering shall set us free. Don't you agree?

That is correct, we dont agree I goes & Nuncles like Purgatory, torture, hell itself I prefer to that which my eyes saw.

But then he thinks about abandoning Cordelia an goes Yet sweet Cordelia… Ye Gods cut my head off with a golden axe, and smile upon the stroke that murders me rather than my wits be jammed in this choice.

His thoughts force him to walk up & down at this point just like & actor would do on stage. But he doesnt stroke his beard.

Do we then accept our inexplicable purgatory on this heath and allow fate to play as it will with Cordelia, Sir? goes Pignut For I am certain that Fate will find a way to lead her by the hand to the mouth of hell if we remain on this heath. I feel it in every morsel of flesh in my bones.

Pox on the heath! Nuncle spits A pox on her green sickness. He looks at me wi one twisted eye takes another step & looks at Pignut wi the other. He puts his hands to his mouth like hes praying blows air from his nose over his fingertips & comes to a decision.

Nay. Nay he goes A father must raise inner armies to save his daughter out of sight of cruel death.

Pignut wipes some rain from her mouth & goes Then we must bestow more thought on the matter because I too do not wish to experience again our recent horrors, Sirs. But I do wish my body heart and mind to be free from the yoke of this moor. In short I wish to make safe return to my *real* life.

And I, Pignut, wish the world to look on my wrongs with an indifferent eye Nuncle goes & he shouts Ye Gods! Power is like a circle in the water, which never ceaseth to enlarge itself till by broad spreading it disperse to nought. How proceed Pignut?

Pignut goes So firstly, to obviate a repeat of our most recent tragedy, I am determined that Kent cannot ride to Dover.

She lifts a hefty hazel branch & wields it like a club & Nuncles like What kill my good servant Kent? Nay. Nay. The heaviness and guilt within my bosom takes off my manhood: I have belied a good man & now thoust would have him murdered?

I do not plan to kill Kent, Sir, goes Pignut Simply subdue him & Nuncles like But what then when his deadlights open? He shalt steer us to tragedy or have fate leap us to horrors worser to those afore come to pass.

Pignut rips out some twine & goes No Sir, we shall fasten him securely and make attempt to impose reason on him. If he can be made to comprehend the seriousness of the situation then, being Kent thy loyal servant, he must feel duty bound to serve his King.

Nuncle thinkwalks then goes You do advance your cunning more and more & shes like Are you ready Sir? & Nuncle goes I am bold with attention & Pignut goes Say the words & Nuncles like No, I will be the pattern of all patience; I will say nothing.

Lightning.   Thunder.

32

ACT III SCENE II. Another part of
the heath. Storm ftill. Enter Kent

Who's there? Kent shouts & Im like Marry, here's grace
and a cod-piece; that's a wise man and a fool & Kent goes Alas,
Sir, are you here? Things that love night love not such nights
as these; the wrathful skies gallow the very wanderers of the
dark.

Before Nuncle can reply Pignut whispers I know you are
Kent & his face is like what the fuck & he goes My Lord, what
is this madness this witch raves? & Nuncle goes All the world's
a stage and all the men and women merely players & Kent
shakes his head & asides It is clear my Lord speaks from a
sickness. I must intelligence Cordelia her father's condition &

fuckyi! Pignut scuds him on the boncebox wi the log &
down he goes like a sack of Shakespearian spuds.

Quickly goes Pignut & we tie Kent to the hazel wi all sorts
of belts twigs twine & strands of wool till hes a tangle of royal
knots. Its like an explosion in a boy scouts convention fuck-

sakes we tied him up wi knots not yet even invented. Blood downran the back of his neck. The bold Pignut had skelped him a wee bit too enthusiastically & I couldnt help feeling this was partly driven by thoughts of Rochester feelings of self-loathing low self-esteem & abandonment. I decided to keep one eye on Pignut prim & proper on the outside & totally ruthless on the inside.

When Kents trussed up like a Guantanamo Bay detainee Nuncle takes a closer look & goes Kent has but a thin disguise as this fellow Caius and yet the King was easily deceived at the first.

Even though the moor has us stuck in eternal time our wait for Kent to regain consciousness has a wee eternity of its own. For that time were buried alive in thoughts of our previous lives. Nuncle in sheer regret Pignut in a lesser regret & me? I am both sickness and antidote in one good to taste hard to swallow pill.

My feet have sunk & inch into the mud by the time Kents semi-conscious & he goes automatically like hes programmed Gracious my Lord, hard by here is a hovel. Some friendship will it lend you 'gainst the tempest & Pignut goes No. Stop. Speak not! Sir, Kent, please stop speaking, desist but Kents like Gracious my Lord, hard by here is a hovel. Some friendship will it lend you 'gainst the tempest & Pignut hits him & almighty slap. Awch!

Wi Kent tied confused & wide eyed we describe to him whats been going on & as we pile over each other recounting alternative realities his head swings from one to the other nodding in agreement. But I can see hes thinking Cant wait to get the fuck outa here away from these psychos & tell Cordelia what kinda clusterfucks going on out there on that heath.

Dost thou believe't? goes Nuncle beaming wi the curvy mouth of friendship.

I have so heard goes Kent And do in part believe. But look, the morn, in russet mantle clad, walks o'er the dew of yon high eastward hill. Break we our watch up; and by my advice let us impart what we have seen to-night to young Cordelia.

There was fuck all dawn coming over no hill. Kent nods at his hands to be freed but Nuncle goes Thou speakest in truth good Caius? & Kents like Heaven be my witness to you my Lord, if you suspect in me any dishonesty & Nuncles about to set him free when I goes Nay Nuncle untie him not. He lies.

Kent slumps back & he wouldve threw his hands up if they werent tied. He goes Am I in earth, in heaven, or in hell? Sleeping or waking? Mad or well-advised?

Well advised good Caius goes Nuncle Thou art well advised by thy King. Listen with good heart. But Kent goes I hold my duty as I hold my soul, both to my God and to my gracious King; and I do think - or else this brain of mine hunts not the trail of policy so sure as it hath us'd to do - that I have been evidenced of the King's lunacy.

Fie! Nuncle goes Fie! Fie! Have the Pelican sisters taught thee to insult? & Kents like Nay my good Lord. Mine eyes and mine ears are my teachers. I alone evidence thy lunacy.

Nuncle goes to Pignut Is there no way in the heavens to change this man's mind?

Leave him here goes Pignut Where he can't interfere & Nuncle smiles wi one eye & turns to me & goes My good boy. Come, bring us to this hovel & theres & almighty

like a Mach three jet & a nuclear light & we tumble jolt & accelerate through space time. Or more correctly we are space time.

33

ACT III SCENE IV. The
heath. Before a hovel

The dilapidated door creaks open & in we tumble.

Fathom and half, fathom and half! says Poor Tom! & I go Tom Tom Bedlam we have your King here and a woman.

Wanderers, Poor Tom hath news from Dover.

Humour him Nuncle says & Pignuts like Dover? Thee hath news from Dover? & Poor Toms like Aye! Thee shalt not defy the foul fiend who still through the hawthorn blows the cold wind: Says suum, mun, ha, no, nonny. Dolphin my boy, my boy, sessa! let him trot by.

Nuncle goes Why, thou wert better in thy grave than to answer with thy un-covered body but I stop the daft old cunt & go Nuncle forget thee the clothes and find the news & as I peer into the night for Gloucesters torch Nuncles like Where-fore Gloucester? & Poor Tom goes. Gloucester is dead my Lord. In the battle at Dover.

Again? goes Nuncle.

Nay my Lord, just this once.

Didst good Lord Caius swift ride to Cordelia? goes Nuncle & Poor Toms like Nay. Caius is dead also. With a hey nonny nonny no.

Caius dead? goes Nuncle. Dead?

Yeah Sirs. Some gang of ragamuffins did rob good Caius and tie him to a tree where he thereupon was ripped apart by a savage pack of Scottish wolves.

Nuncle busts into tears Oh my good Kent. My loyal Kent & Poor Tom goes His last words were Eek! Eek! Then he spoke from out a hole in his throat.

On no. Nay nay. Good Kent nay goes Nuncle I am a darkened Midas. I alchemy friendship into death. All my future decisions contaminated by one mistake.

And Pignut goes What of Cordelia Poor Tom? Does Cordelia live?

Cordelia captured by Goneril and Regan he goes They torture her for pleasure by night and hunt with hounds for the King by day. Fie, foh, and fum, I smell the blood of a British King.

&   were fired to

34

ACT V SCENE III The Brit
iſh camp near Dover.

A screaming Cordelia is lashed to a distant pole. Fire licks its way up her legs. The flames are propelled by buckets of liquefied fat from the melted bodies of French soldiers.

O, horrible! O, horrible! most horrible! goes Nuncle.

Regan and Goneril usher lines of soldiers wi great urns of water to continually douse Cordelias face so she can fully experience the burning of her body. The final object of the intellect – the last object to disappear. Thats why the pain is more than physical & the screams are more than existential. They say a woman can hear her own babys cries even at a Celtic and Rangers game. Cordelias screams pierce every realm of the universe. The Pelican sisters stand pointing & cackling. But Cordelia despite the pain spits in their faces & screams abuse A pox o' your throats, you bawling, blasphemous, incharitable dogs. May your beards burst in flame. Thou art a boil, a plague sore, an embossed carbuncle in my corrupted blood!

Her face was horrible. Idve never thought Cordelia capable of such a face even under terrible pain. In retaliation Regan balances a hot stone on the end of her sword & flips it into Cordelias mouth where it hisses before she spits it through blistering lips & screams A cursed death on you, ye mongrel bitch!

Nuncle runs as fast as a beaten old man can over rotting bodies screaming Butchers and villains! Bloody cannibals! How sweet a plant have you untimely cropp'd!

He wraps himself around Cordelia but the sisters douse him in Frenchmans fat set him alight & applaud the flames like little girls at a magic trick. Nuncle doesnt let go. He holds tighter to Cordelia as the flames rise & goes A father must raise inner armies to save his daughter.

Father & daughter are another grotesque statue in the telling of this tale lit up orange & yellow & red among the jutting dark shadows of the dogs & blasted structures of war.

Nuncle screams Thou elvish-mark'd, abortive, rooting hogs! & Cordelia lets loose wi a barrage of words never before in her mouth she goes Poisonous bunch-backed toad! Come, come forward you unable worms!

Tragedy thwarted will bleed its course somehow & now it was bleeding heavily into Cordelia. Pignut said something like it on the heath.

Regan tims on another liquefied bucket of fat & whoosh all thats left is two heads above the flames their hair sizzling like radioactive candy floss. Theyre still screaming as the flames engulf them so that it looks like screaming flames. Silence except for the laughing sisters.

Then lightning blinds my eyes &

35

returned to the heath (7)

Pignut vomits wi one hand on the tree like a drunk man in an alley. The smell of burning flesh in my hooter tastes sooty on the back of my throat & when Nuncle comes trudging over Ive never seen him so defeated.

A raindrop for a smile good Nuncle I go & his look is neither glare nor stare. Its the look of a man who has lost great power. Two black holes. Were just two lost souls swimming in a fish bowl year after year.

Wish you were here.

Smile I cannot do my boy he goes I do witness the death of my daughter repeated with worser horror. But Boy, Boy, come thee closer, I saw the foul beast in her face when she spat. She has summonsed up evil where none did exist.

Perhaps, Sir, her behaviour was generated by fear goes Pignut.

Anger is fear in a clanging suit of armour, Nuncle I goes & hes like Nay! Hate wast in her glittering eyes, violence of the worst. Cordelia's soul rots on Lethe wharf.

Is your daughter not human, Sir? goes Pignut Is she not entitled to these feelings?

Those of us full burdened by the weary days of life are entitled to hate goes Nuncle For it will corrupt us no more. Hate, anger, even jealousy, her eye is sick on them all. Immaculate and spotless was her mind. Now: sick sick sick!

But you must account, Sir, that this has not in reality transpired goes Jane Lord Kent, on your bidding, has still to appear an she points From this very storm to offer shelter to betake yourself to.

I hear thy words Pignut Nuncle goes But deep in, that part beyond our cognizance, underneath the yoke of reality, in there, he goes & beats his chest like Nuncle Pius XII used to do an goes A voice whispers me my girl is more polluted each time we go forth with best hearts. In short: we condemn, by degrees, that innocent soul.

These are dark imaginings, Sir goes Pignut but Nuncle whips around in anger & goes Ye saw it upon her face!

I saw pain and spasms of agony, Sir! Pignut goes stares at him for one & a half seconds exactly then turns away.

But Nuncle was dead on. In trying to make things right we were fuckin it right up. Like pouring water on a chip pan fire. Or politicians on poverty.

Perhaps I am made for tragedy goes Nuncle To repeat for eternity the issues of my mistakes. Nay! Let Mars divide eternity in twain, set a huge mountain 'tween my heart and tongue. Mine words are tiny devils.

If I may speak, Sirs goes Pignut Our interfering seems to

set off a domino effect well beyond our control, I think we can agree on that point?

One things bumps t'other till the whole Kingdom is at loggerheads goes Nuncle.

Yes Sir she goes Beyond prediction and control.

And? Nuncle goes but Pignut shrugs & wipes some rain from her eyes & goes We need some time to carefully, very, very carefully, ponder the problem.

So we settle to think in the rain. It doesnt really matter how long we sat. I think on the heath we might be outside Spacetime. I rememberd this day I dropped a stone in good faith into a pond to frighten the fish away from a stalking cat. They were beautiful carp over thirty years old & when they turned the light hit their scales like a blacksmiths hammer on hot metal. But when the stone hit the water a duck flapped straight into the claws of a cat. The cat was so pleased wi his luck he dragged the duck in front of a car & became the flat cat of fame. The driver swerved into oncoming traffic & caused a pile up where thirty people died. One for every year of the fish. The duck flew back to the pond & eventually the ripples settled.

Pignut goes Sirs, we should vehemently resist our desire to interfere, preventing as best we can, the effects of our actions on the plot.

I list thee Nuncle goes.

If we could reach Cordelia, in Dover, with the plot unchanged goes Pignut If we could contrive to allow Kent, Gloucester and Poor Tom, to come and go as they should. If we can change as little as *possible*...

Let the afore set tragedy sail us over smoothest waters Nuncle goes And canst this save her soul, Pignut?

If we lay our plans accordingly, we shall speak directly to Cordelia, Sir, and hope that she may, at last, lay down her arms and retreat to France.

Theres a prayer in this silence Nuncle goes & Pignut nods that she is ready & he goes No, I will be the pattern of all patience; I will say nothing and theres the usual lightning &

we hear Kent approach but because we dont interfere except for a few funny looks at Pignut we sail through *King Lear* straight to the French Camp eager to persuade Cordelia.

36

ACT IV SCENE VII. A tent in the French camp. LEAR on a bed afleep

Cordelia appears wi black circles round her eyes & a slight twist now to her spine so that one shoulders drooped. Her elegance limps along. She gawps at Jane & goes What art thou?

Jane taken aback by the state of Cordelia goes I am a servant of the King, good Cordelia but Cordelia grabs her throat & screeches How do thee come by my name. Art thou a British spy?

Jane croaks out I am an ally of the King.

Cordelia releases her grip & goes Where my father?

He is being attended to by a doctor.

Nuncles lying on a makeshift bed pretending to be mad & Im wandering about hiding in plain sight as Fools do.

Wi the tip of her sword Cordelia uppicks the daisy chain Nuncle had filled wi songs & goes He made thus for Regan and Goneril when I was a child. How does my father?

He sleeps for now goes Jane But when he wakes I fear he

shall not know thee.

And thou hast brought my father to yonder bed?

Yes, I have, myself and Mister Fool.

I nod a jingle bell & Cordelias eyes narrow like its the first shes noticed me & she goes Dost thou vouch for this woman Fool?

I do vouch sweet Cordelia.

Didst thou pass the British camp she goes & I jingle side to side bell & Pignuts like No, we travelled here on a much wider radius.

I step in & go I have sadly to inform thee that thy father's mind has burst with grief over banishing his sweetest daughter, good Cordelia.

Cordelia snorts & goes Grieve not, so called father, for thou hast made me strong and I teeter now on the edge of power.

Her fist tightens round the handle of her sword & revenge flashes red in her eyes or else it was the sun going down.

Nuncle approaches trailing the Doctor pleading for him to rest. Cordelias back straightens. Nuncle opens his arms but receives a cold My Lord. Thou art here & he drops his arms & goes Good Cordelia I must beseech thee to flee immediately to France.

Why to France, my Lord, with power almost restored?

Lear takes her by the shoulders & goes To France I say. Thy father, against all odds, will save thy life.

Art thou mad as they are saying thou art? Power is almost restored!

Cordelia, my one daughter, my true daughter, I cannot explain more properly but by the strict'st decrees of the King I order thee to fly to France.

Nay! goes Cordelia Nay! Ha! Thou art no King. These hands, these hands, itch to repair those violent harms that my two sisters have made! Be careful, Sir, lest they itch for thee.

Take heed, lest by your heat you burn yourself Nuncle goes.

Speak truth of it, Sir, thy face says you have so traitorously discovered the secrets of my army and made such pestiferous reports of men very nobly held.

Nay! Nay. There have been portents Nuncle goes & Cordelia swings her sword to Pignut O clock & goes Or Spies!

This woman is no spy, Cordelia goes Nuncle This woman is our saviour & Cordelia coughs up a grogger & spits on Pignuts shoe. Nuncle stares like its blood running from his daughters knifed heart.

What prithee are these portents old man?

Portents, paining me to relate, of impending tragedy.

Thee Cordelia goes to Jane Spy, thou knowest of a portent? Jane nods aye.

And thee Fool?

I jingle bell & she goes to Nuncle Speak then this portent or be treated as spies & hes like Out of the powerful regions beyond earth, there are portents that you shalt be defeated by those Pelican sisters.

Cordelia swings the blade to Nuncle O clock & goes Blood would I draw on thee now if thou weren't my father & Nuncle backsteps & goes Peace sweet child!

Mine hatred for my sisters is so strong victory is assured goes Cordelia You are with me or against me.

Lear blurts out I, myself, thy father, have witnessed these portents, Cordelia. I have suffered them play out their horrors with these tired old eyes.

Thou art mad indeed goes Cordelia & turns to walk away when Nuncle shouts I have held thee in my arms as thou died!

She turns back the gravel rasping under her heels & goes My father imagines his daughter dead?

Nay. Nay. The opposite be true.

Mark how the tyrant speaks she goes Thou banished me, respected me not. And I return, perhaps to break thy necks.

Tis my heart you break, good Cordelia. There is something in't that stings my nature; for it has changed me almost into another man.

If thou art changed to aught, 'tis to an ass she goes & Nuncles like I have seen things fly with truth as wings and these things hath doused the hot coals in my heart.

Cordelia sneers she goes Medicine this silly statesman Physic. He must of necessity be portcullised from his mind.

How does my royal Lord? the Doctor goes but Nuncle pushes him aside & goes You do me wrong to take me as mad Cordelia. You do thyself wrong. The wide Kingdom. We will be bound upon wheels of fire, that your own tears shalt scald like molten lead.

He is far, far wide! goes Cordelia.

I am here goes Nuncle In the centre of fair daylight, serving my daughter warning. Call off the battle.

Look upon me, Sir...

Call off the battle!

Behold the manifestation of revenge goes Cordelia & Nuncle goes I fear it is thou who art not in perfect mind for those are not my Cordelia's eyes.

These eyes are set on revenge.

Nuncle drops to his knees & goes You would have sold your King to slaughter, his princes and his peers to servitude, his subjects to oppression and contempt and his whole kingdom into desolation.

I will revenge or sell my title for a glorious grave, Father.

Then, Cordelia, if you have poison for me, I will drink it. For I hath visioned thy end at the hands of thy sisters and cannot bear witness to more.

Ha! Sisters! Bid farewell to thy daughters, Father in only name, for I shall drink victory's sweet wine goes Cordelia & Nuncle runs his fingertips across the grass tastes the dew & goes The very earth tastes now of death.

This earth shalt soon be mine own kingdom goes Cordelia Now will your highness walk for I shall not bear a grovel for a father.

Nuncle struggles up despairs at me & Pingut then nods. I hold onto my own fist as his voice croaks out You must bear with me. Pray you now, forget and forgive: I am old and foolish.

Lightning.   Electric milk. Bzzz bzzz
& all is suddenly dark.   Were rolling through clouds. Then
falling to the ground wi a thump.

37

ACT V SCENE II. A field be tween the two campſ.

Alarum within. Enter, with drum and colourſ, KING LEAR, CORDE
LIA, and Soldierſ, over the ſtage; and exeunt

We march to war wi the British. We march to the slaughter.

3⁸

ACT V SCENE III The Brit
iſh camp near Dover.

We are hiding amid afterbattle smoke & flame. Down below Cordelias swung by two men an flung into a pit. The baying mob applauds. Regan screams Wrath, envy, treason, rape, and murder's rages. Good sister Goneril cry havoc and let slip the dogs of war!

Goneril admits Edmund & Cornwall into the pit.

Do thy will goes Goneril & as they do their will the soldiers on the edges chant Ho Ho Ho.

Nuncle struggles through mutilated bodies like a man in deep mud. The soldiers applaud & jeer Edmund & Cornwalls every violation & as Nuncle breaks through Regan orders him held. They lash Nuncle belly down on a crucifix at the edge of the pit & hold his eylids open so he cant miss the defilement.

Stop! Halt! Nuncle shouts but the rape continues. Regan whispers to Nuncle Chop off thy hand father and I shalt order halt. Nuncle grunts & without hesitation reaches out for a sword. All eyes in the darkness stare as he lifts the blade.

Cordelia screams Disobey! But, for all this, I would tread upon the tyrants' heads father. Disobey! Disobey!

Let her be silenced Goneril shouts & Cornwall clamps Cordelias tongue wi hot tongs pulls it like tough elastic & slices it off. She spits blood flesh & mangled words in his face. Nuncle chops deep into his left wrist so its hanging only by silver ligaments. White bone in moonlight. Firelit blood squirts onto the grass.

Let her live he screams The deed is done. Ye Gods let her live. Stop! but Regan outsniggers an goes You tedious old fool. The King desires some gentle entertainment. Cornwall. Throw me my baby sister's hands, if you please!

Edmund holds Cordelias arms & Cornwall axes off her hands. One chop each. They sear the blood flow wi a screaming torch flame to the cheers of soldiers.

Nuncle & Cordelia float off into mumbling unconsciousness & Goneril holds up Cordelias hands by the fingertips & goes Now assure they are both baked in that pie wherefore her father daintily shalt feed on the flesh that he himself hath bred.

Pignut vomits on my jingle bells. Theres nothing we can do but wait for the grisly ending. All the pain is real even if we arent.

By the time the skinnymalinky cook returns Pignut has one eye open to see the sisters wake Nuncle wi sharp needles & smelling salts. Goneril goes Do thou one thing father and thy sweetest Cordelia shalt live. Do it not and Cornwall shall draw her bowels like rope wi her awaked wi medicine to witness.

Cornwall holds a surgeons razor against Cordelias belly. A single trickle of blood runs sideways down her waist. Nuncle lashes out but hes tied wi such ropes & held by such men & weakened by such sorrow that hes ineffectual as a kitten in a drowning bag. Regan drifts the pie under his nose & goes Eat ye this pie and your sweet, sweet, Cordelia lives.

Eat… eat a pie? goes Nuncle surprised & suspicious. He peers around clump after clump of intense eyes leaning over him. Towering over him. A cave a tent of eyes like a mushroom trip. Protruding. Eager.

Yeah! Eat thou this pie and Cordelia shall live in dumbery & stumpery. But if thou refuse she will be drawn. Her screams to her father shall be weird music and death you'll wish upon her.

In nights of madness senseless maketh sense Nuncle goes & grunts Aye. The King shall eat. A soldier props him on one elbow & offers the pie to his mouth.

Nuncle tries to bite into the crust but his mouth has dried wi rage & terror & he goes Water & a greasy goblet of victory wine is thrust to his lips. He gobbles it down but some thirsts are unquenchable. When he chews & swallows the mob cheer & poke their weapons into the red sky.

The whole pie shall be eaten Goneril goes & Nuncle grunts for more. Each time he swallows a cheer goes up. When hes finished he goes Oh let her live!

Didst thee enjoy the fare father?

Nuncle stares.

Now wasn't that a handy-dandy dish to lay before the king? Hark, the soldiers snigger!

The sniggering soldiers puzzle Nuncle & he goes Hath thou poisoned me? Ha! I thank thee for I welcome poison as ambrosia.

Nay. Thou old fool. Not poison.

If not poison then why mock foul Pelican? Why laugh thy mercenaries?

For my dearest father, thou hast eaten thy daughter's hands she goes & a great mocking roar bends the scorched grass where me & Pignut lay.

O heat, dry up thy brains! Tears seven times salt burn out the sense and violence of thine eye! By heaven, thy madness shall be paid by weight till our scale turn the beam goes Nuncle & vomits into the blood saturated earth.

I think the King will fast before he buys again at such a price goes Regan 'Twas full of gristle; doth thee like the taste?

Nuncle vomits again. Sick sticks to his beard like a drunken madman.

Goneril nods & one soldier holds Nuncle up by the hair while another holds his eyelids open by the lashes to witness Cordelia squeak sheer agony as Cornwall slices open her belly and her entrails push out like a cooked haggis. He digs in wi both hands like a baker kneading dough & piles her steaming entrails onto her breasts. Cordelia expels a sustained high pitched groan.

Edmund flaps away some croaking battlefield rooks. Even

from this distance I see the delicious shine of evil in the Pelican sisters eyes.

Why is mankind such instrument of evil? Pignut goes & breaks down crying.

I suppose its cos your egos relationship wi the will to live is exaggerated or bolstered or strengthened in some way by witnessing death & the more horrible the death the closer your ego feels to immortality. But its the will to live thats eternal. Were just the fuckin vessels us & our egos. When that vessel pops like a bubble in an Irn Bru bottle your portion finds another vessel. Or vessels. Grass trees stones birds or wolfs. Thats how Ive always been a vegetarian.

Anyway as Pignut sobs into her hands existence departs Cordelia to seek out another vessel. Nuncle vomits up his own heart. Its swinging from his mouth on the end of its own veins & arteries coated wi blood & slabbers. It beats three times

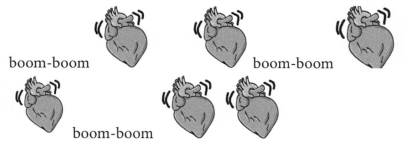

boom-boom   boom-boom

boom-boom

& stops.

Theres a new silence. A silence that becomes eerie. Even the soldiers are uneasy. The Pelicans fill the night wi shrieks of laughter.

Lightning blinds my eyes &

39

returned to the heath (8)

The wind makes stinging whips from our clothes. The stones have a brooding presence like theyve been awaiting our return. That sensation you sometimes get when theres such a silence you sense consciousness in inanimate things. But its existence stupid. Theres a conduit from one existing object to another. Were all the one thing & for that moment youre seeing things as they are in themselves. Then your erroneous sense of self snaps you from true bliss back to existential loneliness.

Pignut & Nuncle retch sour nothings onto the heather. Nuncle wipes his slabbers & swears he can still taste the terrible pie on his lips & Pignuts like It's not real, It's not real, this is not real to herself.

But it is real. Was real. Will be real. Cos all things imagined dreamed hallucinated past present & future & dreams are as real as each other. We are watchers forever offset from the one true reality by one millimetre of ego.

Nuncle goes Oh Pignut, the multiplying villainies of nature do swarm upon my mind. My fairest daughter murdered horrible and worse. Boy. Boy! My heart is burst, Cordelia hath lost half her soul. Even now, now, very now, the old horned ram is topping my white ewe.

Nuncle slumps into the wet heather & curls up. I curl beside him & softly go But it hath not come to pass, Nuncle. Tis all but a troubled dream. Shht. Shht.

See here afore ye, on this heath, a King transformed to a gnat! he goes O Boy, my Boy, the dream's here still: even when I wake, it is without me, as within me; not imagined, felt. I could be bounded in a nutshell and count myself a king of infinite space, couldst I believe these are but bad dreams.

But Mister Fool is right, Sir, goes Pignut For in the illogical logic of this heath, even though I have no wish to repeat it, all we have experienced, terrible though it be, beyond terrible, has, in truth and logic, not yet happened.

Nuncle goes I have come to love thee as a daughter these past times Pignut, yet thou salvest me not for I must think of murders, rapes and massacres, acts of black night, abominable deeds, complots of mischief, treason, villainies ruthful to hear, yet piteously perform'd: and this all be forever in my mind, unless thou swear to me my child, Cordelia, shall, even if she dies, be still pure.

Instead of answering tears outcome Pignuts eyes & her pity for Nuncle shudders her body.

Cans't thou save Cordelia's soul Pignut Nuncle goes From the claws of the foul beast?

Sir Pignut goes Perhaps, once well rested, if you so wished

and did choose by your own will, I might regain the fortitude to have one final attempt to achieve Cordelia's safety. If we fail then I am resigned to spend eternity in this abominable place.

Yeah?

Yes. And perhaps Mister Fool is of a similar opinion?

Boy?

If thou wert my fool, Nuncle, I'd have thee beaten for being old before thy time I goes & helps him up.

Thank you boy.

Nuncle I goes Let us find out the prettiest plot we can, and make the bitter Pelicans, with our pikes and partisans, a grave.

Do you mean kill them? goes Jane & Im like I think I do Pignut.

Nuncle sighs out his nose. It could be resignation or approval.

Who cannot be crushed with a plot? he goes.

We get our bonceboxes together & think a million plots & plans to rid ourselves & the world of the horribles & at the end Nuncle goes Thus we are agreed?

Wed pad easy through the tragedy upsetting nothing. Tread the same blades of grass our cheeks to the same side of the breeze. Wed acquiesce to Kent leading us to the hovel. Humour Poor Tom to the heights of his feigned madness. Go meekly wi Gloucester to the Farmhouse. Arrive in Dover wi Nuncle pretending perfect madness. March wi alarum drum & colours to war. But once the battle commences well sneak like sailors of the night from the battlefield. Well find Goneril & Regan & cut their throats.

Nuncle takes a long steady inbreath we brace & he goes
No, I will be the pattern of all patience; I will say nothing

Flash.

40

ACT IV SCENE VII. A tent in the French camp. LEAR on a bed afleep

From a cluster of drunk & singing soldiers Cordelia appears swigging from a bottle. Her lips pop separating from the glass. Thats when I see her teethve rotted to stumps. Shes got black circles round her eyes one shoulder drooped & bald patches on her head. She looks like a buckie slurping post-apocalyptic Glasgow Ned.

Her mouth wide like a cartoon she fires a drunken volley at Pignut she goes What art thou weird slut? laughs takes another swig & goes Where got'st thou that goose look? Ha! Mend your shoes!

Staying on plan Pignut goes I am a servant of the King, good Cordelia but Cordelia claws her throat spits in her face & screeches How dost thee come by my name triple-turn'd whore! Art thou a British spy?

Good Cordelia goes Pignut wiping spit wi her cuff I mean no offence I am a true friend and an ally of the King.

The King? The King? Hail, great king! I sour your happiness with horse-piss. Where is that filthy beggar, pox of wrinkles?

He is being attended by a doctor Pignut goes But shall arrive shortly.

Bring my father hither or face my wrath Cordelia barks & two rough as fuck soldiers march off quickstep doubletime fear tingling the soles of their feet.

Wi the tip of her sword Cordelia uppicks the daisy chain Nuncle had filled wi songs & goes My *father* made this dross for Regan and Goneril when I was a child. She flicks it in the air & slices it twice swish swish before it falls then brings the weight of her sword to rest on Pignuts sternum & goes Didst thou pass the British camp scurvy whoredaughter?

No. No miss, we travelled here on a much wider radius.

Cordelia narrows her sunken eyes at me & goes Dost thou vouch for this woman Fool?

I do vouch good Cordelia and have sadly to inform thee that thy father's grief, over banishing his sweetest daughter, hath burst the buckles of his mind. I plead thee treat the old Banbury cheese kindly.

Cordelia snorts & goes A curse my noble father laid on me, when he did crown my sisters' warlike brows with wide skirted meads and mellow streams. And with their scorns drew rivers from these eyes! But grieve not finch-egg for these wrongs have made me strong and I teeter now on the edge of power.

Her fist tightens on the hilt of her sword her knuckles a

row of tainted pearls & revenge flashes in her eyes when two soldiers return wi Nuncle.

Cordelias back straightens. Her nostrils flare & one side of her top lip lifts. Nuncle opens his arms & goes Greetings good Cordelia but shes a statue carved from hate & granite. Nuncles arms flop like wet spaghetti & he goes Good Cordelia I am here to advise thee in thy wars so that thy place shall be made honourable.

Why my Lord, Cordelia goes then takes a swig Why my Lord, unless you could teach me to forget a banished daughter, you must not learn me how to fight my battles.

Lear takes her by the shoulders & goes Let a father undo his wrongs but she pushes away going Prithee, hic, father, tell why thou dost arrive with power almost restored?

You see me here, Cordelia Nuncle goes A poor old man, as full of grief as age; wretched in both. Doubt not but heaven hath brought me to your command in this just war.

Nay. Nay she goes Cordelia fool no more. Prithee listen well old man. When I spy advantage, I'll claim the crown, for that's the golden mark I seek to hit. Nor shall tyrant father usurp my right, nor hold the sceptre from my fist. Cordelia shalt wear the diadem upon her head she goes & crowns her porridge box doink wi an imaginary diadem.

Cordelia, my only true daughter, my one daughter, I am at your command as are my companions Nuncle goes but Cordelia points her sword at Pignut & goes Companions father? Or Spies?

This woman is no spy Nuncle goes This woman is our

salvation, body and soul.

Cordelia splits Pignuts skirts crotch to floor wi the sword & goes Strumpet, art thou a spy?

Most certainly I am not. I am an ally goes Pignut gathering together the cloths of dignity. Cordelia raises the sword tip to Pignuts throat & goes Ay; it is not a language thou speakest. Art – thou – a spy?

As I have said miss, if you would do me honour in listening…

Do thee honour? Do thee honour Tawdry Whore?

Cordelias goanny push the sword through so I blurt out There have been portents good Cordelia! & she swings her sword to me & goes Holla, you clown! Dost thou know of a portent?

I jingle bell & shes like Speak then this portent all-licens'd fool, or fresh tortures I'll invent for thee.

These are powerful portents that… that… with your father's assistance you shall defeat your Pelican sisters.

My father's assistance?

Yeah good Cordelia.

Horse piss Cordelia goes an swishes her blade to Nuncles throat & goes Blood would I draw on thee if thou weren't my father & Nuncle backsteps & goes Peace sweet child of mine! We are well foretold of thy victory and forthwith shut the gates for safety of ourselves; for now we owe allegiance unto Cordelia.

Uncle bows & me & Pignut follow suit. Cordelia takes a long tug at the bottle smashes it casually on a rock & yelps

Keep ye watch on these spies comrades. On moonrise we battle!

Cordelia marches off wi her phalanx of drunken soldiers leaving two watching over us. Nuncle gives us his signal. Pignut steadies herself. I dig my fingers into the earth & he croaks after Cordelia You must bear with me. Pray you now, forget and forgive: I am old and foolish.

As Cordelia turns her face is washed by lightning.

BOOM!

Electric milk. Bzzz bzz. Dark. Rolling through clouds. Elevated. Falling.

ACT V SCENE II. A field be
tween the two campſ.

Alarum within. Enter, with drum and colourſ, KING LEAR, CORDE
LIA, and Soldierſ, over the ſtage; and exeunt

We find ourselves marching wi squadrons of French soldiers. Leaves hurtle wi fleeing birds over the tops of straining
pikes & swords. Thumping boots. Soldiers soldier onto other
soldiers soldiering on to them. Into the mouth of war these
soldiers march leaving behind lovers mothers & dreaming
children. Wide eyed they go & in that gap between dumping
each moment & hoping for the next theyll find the absolute
clarity of being where imminent death has washed away the
veil between them & things as they actually are.

Halt! cries Cordelia from a spirited white stallion.

A hundred yards off Goneril & Regan pace the British
ranks on unkempt steeds. Three horses of the apocalypse are
there. The fourth one munching grass nearby. Everything
stops & in the silence the soldiers breath.

DES DILLON

Up goes a shout & the British charge. As the French make ready we sneak slinky sideways into the forest & as we creep through the woods animals & deserters scatter from the raging battle. It sounds like a steelwork mixed wi a football match. Nuncles experience of warcraft has us evade forest sentries & outflank till were well behind British lines. Shape, shine, shadow, silhouette, spacing and movement Nuncle goes & learns us how to slither unseen wi grass & twigs in our hair. We come up on their camp from behind. The greased tents are lined up like some pathetic circus.

Just as Nuncle predicted the Pelican sisters had cowered back to camp as the battle commenced & there they would await the horns of victory cos there were their two horses munching mud. We slud closer sometimes running in soft ground sometimes crawling on our bellies to avoid the slashing light of the moon until we came to a tent that had Queen Goneril daubed on the side in blood.

Shadows of seduction flicker on the canvas.

Come, come, you wasp; i' faith, you are too angry goes Edmunds voice & Gonerils like If I be waspish, best beware my sting.

My remedy is then, to pluck it out goes Edmund & he thrusts his hand up her skirts faster than Donald Trump but she spins away & giggles & hes like Oh ho! Albany does well to have a woman like thee.

Albany? goes Goneril throwing herself back onto the mattress The fool couldn't find it where it lies.

Lady, shall I lie in your lap? goes Edmund & she giggles

178

& goes No, my Lord & hes like I mean, my head upon your lap? Do you think I meant country matters? & Goneril goes I think nothing, my Lord & hes like That's a fair thought to lie between maids' legs.

What is, Edmund?

Nothing.

Thou can have nothing if noting thou wants.

Edmund leaps onto the bed beside her. Theres the bulk of one shadow incarnate the rustle & rip of clothes & the popping of buttons & Edmund goes Who knows not where a wasp does wear his sting? In his tail?

In his tongue goes Goneril.

What, with my tongue in your tail? Come good Goneril; I am a gentleman. That I'll try.

Goneril lifts her skirts & pushes his head down to her nothing & when shes lost in moaning we slice & burst through the canvas blades drawn. Edmunds head pops up from between her legs. His eyes swivel from ecstasy to surprise as Nuncle runs him through. He lets out a moan that could be an orgasm if you never seen the sword.

Ohaaah!

Nuncle withdraws & does him again. This time Goneril screams. Edmund slumps to the ground & goes Lear?

Yeah. Lear, thy King! goes Nuncle & slits his throat. The blood pumps out in slices.

Goneril tries to escape but Pignut clunks her on the boncebox wi a handy shillelagh she picked up in the woods. She getting quite good at that. She ties Gonerils hands & I tie her legs & we give her Chinese burns nips & smelling salts till she regains consciousness. Once shes fully awake Nuncle goes Scream not or I slice out thy entrails and pile them on thy chest as thou watchest.

Goneril nods accordance & Nuncle invades her breathing & goes Where is thy sister?

Sir, goes Goneril I love you more than words can wield the matter; Dearer than eyesight, space, and liberty; Beyond what can be valued, rich or rare…

Nuncle hits her a colossal slap & goes Thy silence I crave but she starts again automatic As much as child e'er lov'd, or father found; A love that makes breath poor, and speech unable. Beyond all manner of so much I love you.

Nuncle pins down her arm & chops off her hand & as she screams he Desdemonas her wi a pillow & her scream is muffled & lost in the rage of battle & while Pignut ties a tourniquet I cauterise the wound wi a hot coal. All the while Edmunds dead eyes stare up at us so I drop the hot coal in his open mouth to check hes dead. He is. Not unless he speaks a language called Hiss.

Nuncles removes the pillow allows Goneril to breathe again & goes Where is thy sister fat guts?

She is dead, dying. Dead my Lord.

Dead, dying which? Nuncle goes & Gonerils like I have poisoned her for she is the Chief architect and plotter of these woes father.

Where is she? Nuncle growls & his bear like demeanour is returning.

The villain lies in the very next tent Goneril goes & shouts Discharge thy rage on her as Nuncle slides out the gaping slash in the canvas.

Cordelia pleads wi me & Pignut to let her free. Offers untold power & riches but as Nuncle had trained us we stare at the slash till his return dragging Regan by the feet her hair & arms trailing behind. She gets three colossal slaps & when she kneels up she seems more drunk than poisoned but shes defo puzzled to see us. Puzzledtaefuck.

Good morrow I say with a cheeky as fuck wee wave.

Eh? she goes & when she realises its Nuncle whos dragged her from sleep she tries the same automatic tactics as Goneril.

Sir, she goes I am made of the self-same metal that my sister is but Nuncle goes Of this I am well learnt & punches her to the floor where she lands face to face wi Edmund's body his throat opened like a blood purse. She screams stands & flings herself at Goneril shouting Be not familiar with him. Be not familiar with him!

She strangles Goneril & Pignut makes a move to stop her but Nuncle blocks her & goes Let them be & when Goneril is kinda purplish & eyes bulging Nuncle lifts Regan throws her on the floor at my feet & goes Tie her.

Thy strength hast retuned Nuncle I goes & as I tie Regan up Goneril splutters out a coughing laff & goes Oh sister, I have my revenge afore thy attack for I have not only fobbed thy husband but have, this very evening, poisoned thy cups.

Ha goes Regan I hath long suspected thee of such tricks sister and so, when offered by thy bony hand, I seemed to drink but did not. I ministered the poison back to thee. A sickness grows upon thee sister.

Goneril focuses her attention inwards then goes Sick, Oh Sick. O father have mercy & find me the antidote.

Thou tell'st me what thoust seest in mine eye? goes Nuncle & Goneril goes I see mercy most gracious father. Heavenly mercy.

Nay Pelican daughter. Nay. Thou see'st murder in mine eye.

A father shall not murder his daughters goes Regan.

I have but one daughter he goes Now who dies first? Do thou choose Regan.

Then I choose kill my sister first father.

It shall be done goes Nuncle & draws his sword but it clashes instanter wi another & theres Cordelia hair matted skin glossed wi blood teeth a grinning row of badly tended tombstones like a Louisiana swampland crack head.

Dost thou draw on me father? goes Cordelia nose to nose wi Nuncle Dost thou draw on me?

Nay, Nay. My aim was to murder these shrill shrieking Pelican sisters.

Thou hast left the battle, father and foxed to here. I did suspect thee spies and now tis true-confirmed.

Quick as a flash into opportunity Goneril goes Father, I wish'd to-day our enterprise might thrive but I fear our purpose is discovered & laughs. But her laughter is cut short as

Cordelia knocks her clean out boof wi the hilt of her sword. Her jaw swelling as she snores.

And thee sister? goes Cordelia Needs thou speak to my sword hilt? Nay? The point perhaps? & Regan crawls backwards to the feet of a soldier who on Cordelias nod garrottes her till shes unconscious.

& then its all black for me too & I have a wee trip around eternity where I get to view phenomenalism from the other side & how stunted & brutal it looks. Restrictive. Meaningless. Totally fuckin meaningless. All the egos swimming in it like shoals of piranhas. Insatiable needs & greeds & facebook feeds.

When I come to the French have won the day & I get a rising feeling of elation like we done it! It worked! It fuckinwell worked! Cordelia lives. Cordelia is saved!

But then in the light of a bonfire lines of British soldiers swear allegiance to Queen Cordelia. Refusers are tossed some silent others spitting abuse into the flames. The air is rank wi burning flesh. My ears unmumble Cordelia asking if the spies are awake & thats when I realise Me Pignut & Nuncle are tied up like pigs for the slaughter.

Queen Cordelia approaches & goes Father I would like thee and thy spies to witness raw revenge on thy preferred daughters afore I deal with thee.

They are not mine preferred daughters, you art goes Nuncle & Cordelia smirks shakes her head & shouts Soldiers!

Were roughed up manhandled & shuffled to where Cordelia has Regan & Goneril strapped naked to plinths. Both plinths are tilted inwards so the sisters can witness each others torture.

Goneril, some sweet antidote I have fed goes Queen Cordelia Both sisters eyes bright now with life, I will now raze out the written troubles of mine brain and cleanse the stuff'd bosom of that perilous stuff which weighs upon my heart.

The soldiers cheer.

The Queen places her dagger between Gonerils big & fourth toe & slices down her metatarsals sawing as she goes. Goneril screams & screams & screams. Regan shouts Cordelia, sweet, young, Cordelia hast thee forgotten we art thy sisters.

A sisterly gift then to thee goes the Queen & pushes the blade through the sole of Regans foot this time ripping upwards taking a toe off as she goes.

Fie, thou seemst to have lost a toe sister.

Regans shrieks are drowned by the jeers of the soldiers. Her mouth fills wi night time.

Queen Cordelia holds the toe in the air like a trophy. Blood drips to her hand. She has the stage to herself & moves around well. She goes Gentlemen, I have devised fell tortures for my faults sisters. Strange tortures never before heard of. Behold some tricks I have learned these past times. Physician! Bring thy bag.

The soldiers let out a long pantomime Ooh.

The physician approaches & rolls out a leather bag of blades & instruments on Regans plinth. Regans eyes squint in terror. The dreadful shapes are made even more terrible by reflected flames & the audible interest of the soldiers.

Have mercy sister goes Regan but the Queen ignores her & goes Goneril, thou canst witness thy younger sister receive the selfsame torture thee shalt be dealt in time, so be thy torture doubled, or trebled if ye love her.

Queen Cordelia removes a tiny spoon-shaped blade & goes Fellows, firstly revenge for good Gloucester. Hold fast the whore's head. Regan, upon these eyes of thine I'll set my foot.

Regan screams & her body vibrates as the Queen presses the spoonblade onto the cheekbone & wi one deft flick slices out an eyeball. Blood shoots up falls & wets Regans face. Pignut faints. Regan screams. Queen Cordelia flicks the eyeball up catches it in her mouth wi a gulp that reminds me of a pelican & spits it into her palm.

An extra jelly to better see the future, sister she goes & leans over & jabs her blade into Gonerils thigh & stuffs the eye into its new socket. Each time Gonerils thigh muscle contrast the eye squints.

The spits of hell to thee goes Goneril The devils whore thou shalt be & Queen Cordelias like Her new eye is sick. Observe now the Queen's new learned talents, so named sister.

The place hushes as she takes her time selecting a new blade.

Thou wast always proud of thy legs good sister Regan and rightly so. For they have entangled more men than thou deserved. Let us therefore see what maketh so pretty a leg's component parts.

She signals & her men grip Regans leg. She makes a swift & professional cut around the thigh just below the fud. Regan winces but its only when the Queen digs her dirty nails into the cut & forces her fingers between skin & muscle that Regan screams. The Queen pulls & tugs & rips the skin. Some of the soldiers look away. When the skinning is halfway down the thigh Regan passes out. Her Majesty leaves it like a half removed boot & orders Regan brought back to consciousness wi salts an medicines but when Regan sees her skinboot she falls back into darkness. Queen Cordelia selects pincers & twists at Regans teeth till the painbright brings her around.

Mercy sister. Mercy Regan spits.

I am no sister I am thy Queen she goes taking Regans head off wi a grunt & one swing of her sword. Goneril screams No! No! No!

Queen Cordelia sloshes her hand up inside Regans bloody neck like a ventriloquists dummy & goes in Regans voice Good morrow good Queen Cordelia. How fares thee?

& she laffs.

Oh my daughter has gone to the devil goes Nuncle Cordelia finally possessed by the foul beast.

The Queen continues impersonating Regan. Wobbling her lips wi her fingers she goes Sir, I am made of the selfsame metal that my sister is, and prize me at her worth. In my true heart I find she names my very deed of love.

Goneril screams in existential terror & the Queen places Regans head on Gonerils belly an goes Look sister, Men, wives and children stare, cry out and run as it were doomsday.

Wi her soldiers help Queen Cordelia skins both of Gonerils thighs. This time she rips the skin all the way down to the ankle making sure the physician keeps Goneril conscious & when shes lost in sobs and quiet cries of agony the Queen beats her to death wi Regans head.

Wi each sickening thud Gonerils moans soften. The cracking of skulls & smattering of blood & brains silence even the hardest soldiers & in that eerie quiet the laughing Queen chops off Gonerils head. She pushes a hand into each neck & performs a slow rhythmic dance around the fire. Pagan like.

Hu Hu Hu

she goes & commands the men to join in.
Ha! Ha! Ha!

Hu Hu Hu

Ha! Ha! Ha!

Silhouetted in the bonfire the Queen sings She is dead and gone, lady, she is dead and gone. At her head a grass-green turf, at her heels a stone & then starts humming some nonsense.

By this time Nuncles worked free from his shackles & makes a dash for Queen Cordelia & wraps himself around her going Howl, howl, howl, howl! O, you are men of stones: Had I your tongues and eyes, I'd use them so that heaven's vault should crack. She's gone for ever! I know when one is dead, and when one lives; She's dead as earth.

Nuncle displays immense strength as the soldiers prise him free & when he falls back on his arse Queen Cordelia sets about him in frenzy wi the heads shouting Die thou? Die thou? Thou bastardly rogue! Murder, murder! I am in love with murder!

She hammers him bang wi one head then the other. At

each thumping blow Nuncle stuns & regains himself & as he steadies himself to get to his feet she strikes him again & when he gives up Cordelia beats her father to death.

Light.

returned to the heath (9)

Crawling dripping from his puddle Nuncle goes Boy give me thy clothes.

My clothes Nuncle?

Yeah he goes Thou canst have mine.

Tis a naughty night Nuncle. To swim in.

Cordelia by my actions is abused, stol'n from me, and corrupted by spells and medicines and witchcraft. Hand me thy clothes!

Nay Nuncle, Nay I goes but hes like Make me the fool that I be. Hand me thy clothes.

Nothing hath changed Nuncle I goes We were witness to nothing. A simple nightmare tis all.

Boy. Boy! What fates impose, even Kings must needs abide. It boots not to resist both wind and tide. By saving Cordelia's body I serve her soul to the Fiend he goes & Ive got fuck all to say to that cos its true. There are things beyond us we can never understand but we see the affects back in our world & call them wonder.

There is always a solution, Sir Pignut goes but her eyesre tired & she doesn't believe her own words. Nuncle puts a hand on her shoulder. A tight little smile appears on one side of his mouth & he goes Sweet Pignut, lovely Pignut, tis over. Tis ended. I thank you for your honest care. Clothes boy! For in this tragedy King Lear is the Fool.

Nay Nuncle, I refuse. Tis a naughty night.

Nuncle looks to the naughty night inbreathes deep opens his arms wide & goes Oh Fates Impose me to what penance your invention can lay upon my sin.

Ye sinn'd not Nuncle I goes But in mistaking the hollow clumps and echoes of Pelican beaks for love.

Nay, Nay boy. Arrogance bade me see love in hollow beaks and raw ambition. Tyranny bade me banish innocence to perdition. The fault, all this, lies with me alone. Give me thy clothes or I shall go naked for my sins and for eternity be dying with cold.

Mister Lear, your Majesty goes Pignut The present has many faces to it, has it not? And one should consider all, before pronouncing an opinion as to its nature. Perhaps we should rest for a while, for a great while and then, with sounder minds, we might reconsider our position.

Nay good daughter, for in this heart thou art now my daughter, nay. I shall dress as a Fool and shiver in my puddle eternal rather than worsen the consequences of the world.

Pignut takes Nuncles hand & goes It is possible to believe that, without our intervention, Cordelia could be frozen like an image in a painting, a book never read. Time has stopped and her world and all things in it, become a statue that no one will ever see.

Cordelia frozen?

Yes Sir, if time were to stop nothing could change, all would be frozen.

Frozen in a moment sans forever Nuncle goes & his eyes glaze over an he goes I favour this over Fate's sick pleasures afore shown to us. Father and daughter shall pause for all time, Cordelia a statue feeling nothing, me in a cage of guilt. Hand me thy clothes boy.

I sigh an okay. Pignut doesn't turn away as we swap clothes. Nuncles like an overgrown schoolboy on his first walk home in the rain. The shoes are so tight his feet burst out like dough as he teeters back to his puddle. His clothes trail off me. Im like a walking jumble sale & every second step I trip & fuckin curse.

Behold the shrunken king! I shout but nocunt laffs. I suppose size isnt everything.

If laughter exists on this moor thats when Im sitting looking at the stones wondering if theyre sitting looking at me. The trees too. Im looking at the thing thats inside the trees. Inside the stones & the thing thats inside Pignut & the thing thats inside Nuncle. The driving force of the universe & Im wondering what does it think of all this? Is it inconsequential or is there a plan behind or beyond Beyond & what of this body covered in the glad rags of gold & power? One second the Fool next the King. Such is life. My body might not be anything like flesh and bone. I mean theres the body I perceive & then theres the body for real - the body as it actually is. Then theres the thing that gives consciousness to the body as it actually is. The thing that were part of but can never contact. Thats what causes the absurdification of life. Thats what makes Fools of us all. Fools for worrying. Fools for thinking anything is of consequence. Fools for not believing in reunification and peace.

Then I got to thinking if I could make contact wi that thing I could mibbi change our situation. So I go in deep. I leave the heath & storm & the rain & go past the contemplation of forms & substance till Im in blackness. Nothingness. Then as Im about to give up I see a pinhead of *stuff* appearing & creating actual space & actual time as it grows & Im saying Hello! Hello? but it seems indifferent to me. Indifferent that is till it fuckin engulfs me & I feel... I feel... I feel this feeling that I cant explain. But it was good. It was *the* good. The good that lies behind good. The full good. Good as it actually is. The one & only Good.

I open my eyes cos I hear Pignut shouting No I will be the pattern of all patience; I will say nothing.

She shouts it over & over pausing to listen for some kinda effect. Nuncle goes Pignut, Pignut! Let it be. I shall bedfellow eternity as a Fool. Spoil not my resolve with false hope.

Hope, Sir? goes Pignut my hopes has faltered and I fear I am to be just one more consequence of your actions.

Pignut, goes Nuncle his voice softer than velvet on the back of your leg I love thee as a daughter. Nay, I do love thee now as mine only daughter. My rash faults make serious price of trivial things, creating worlds of chaos but I am not the fault of thy lamentable plight. That cause sparked in thon other world from whence thou camest.

Nuncle takes Pignuts hand kisses it & goes I prithee find thy true path good Pignut. Now let a Fool slumber perchance to dream, for an atom of dreams is a candle of love in this black night.

The gravel crunches & grinds as he curls into a rain soaked Foolcloth ball breathing intermittent ripples over the puddle surface against the force of the wind.

We wait in darkness. I think time passes. I think it does then Pignut goes in a kinda whisper Mister Fool may I speak with you?

Im sure I see a tear on her cheek.

Thou canst speak to thy King I go & over she comes sits down an goes It seems Nuncle is repentant.

Aye. Both kings I go and shes like His eye wandered, and had meaning in its wandering: this gave him an odd look, such as I never remembered to have seen. He is repentant! That must mean something to the Gods or whomever, whatever, controls this place, this world or worlds, these forces.

I shrug my big wet kingly shoulders & Pignut goes Since this seems to be an ending of sorts and since I seem to have been caught up in your world, rather than you in mine, and furthermore caught up against my will, I should logically be freed at some point soon?

Perhaps it is by metaphysics thee shalt free thyself I go For thy faults have brought thee here and so by logic thy faults cannot travel you back.

I beg your pardon Mister Fool? I don't quite understand she goes & Im like You are an umbrella I go & she narrows her eyes & I go What travels up a chimney down but can't travel down a chimney up? & shes like I think I understand & I'm like Ye came here bristled out like a Dilophosaurus and perhaps these bristles must needs be closed for you to travel back.

Go on: what fault do you find with me, pray? she goes & I go The woman who walked onto this heath is not the woman who can walk back off.

I take your point, Mister Fool, but how? How do I physically walk off this heath?

An unexamined life is not worth living I go & she snorts a wee laff & backnods at Nuncle & goes Nuncle's self-examination has destroyed him & Im like No. No. Nuncle hath not yet ended his examination. Destruction is but temporary. His physic is plagued but his metaphysic lights up flights of angels all around.

Pignut shakes her head huffs out a cloud of breath an goes Flights of angels! & Im like Pignut, examine thyself & she folds her arms walks to the tree & sits. I get back to sweetly contemplating what Nuncle Arthur & Nuncle Immanuel learned me.

Pignuts breathing slows. She looks like shes sleeping even though her eyesre open & sometimes moving. Shes like that for hours or weeks or years & then theres this lull in the storm. The moor falls still & the stonesre painted wi moonlight. Pignut opens her eyes & tilts her head like shes heard something. She swings her head about eyes flicking left & right up &

down like shes in some kinda acid trip O God! what is it? she goes Where is it? It does not seem in this room—nor in this house—nor in this garden. It does not come out of the air—nor from under the earth—nor from overhead. But I heard it—where, or whence, for ever impossible to know! And it is the voice of a human being—a known, loved, well-remembered voice—that of Edward Fairfax Rochester; and it speaks in pain and woe, wildly, eerily, urgently.

I am coming! Wait for me! Oh, I will come! she shouts. Nearly shat myself.

Even Nuncle stirred in his puddle asked for quiet & crawled off into the heather.

Pignut stands & moves onto the heather.

Where are you? she screams & theres an echo & Im thinking thats strange an echo bouncing off nothing.

Then she shouts again.

Down superstition! Ah ha! It is my time to assume ascendency. My powers are in play and in force.

Pignut falls to her knees & she penetrates a Mighty Spirit. Her soul rushes out in great luminous wisps & waves pulsating vibrating lighting up the heath in ethereal pinks & blues & yellows. Fuckin amazing. Our own wee Aurora Borealis. Im mesmerised. Im peering directly into the thing that lies behind all things. Then woomph! It comes to abrupt stop & she stands breathing heavily then screams wi volume & authority

Rochester! Rochester! I am sorry I am sorry I am sorry.

43

a man you dont meet every day

Pignut falls out or down or up from that ethereal world regains her bearings turns to me & I goes Did'st thou examine?

She nods her nog & Im like And find thee some truth? & she goes Yes. I am abandoned.

Silly says me Thou canst only abandon thyself Pignut an shes like Then I am abandoned, Mister Fool, by my pig headed adherence to false ideas of morality.

Nay!

Yes.

Nay!

Yes!

Nay Pignut, for thou are abandoned because thou hast esteemed thyself no better than a poor and loathsome beggar unworthy of this Rochester fellow.

Thunk! That arrow hits home & Pignut looks me in the eye without malice & goes I've been a fool.

I let her wander to her stone where she weeps. She weeps

a long long time & I fall asleep or fall into another reality & while Im in there investigating the interface between what is known and what is not known Im pulled back by an emergency call deep in the centre of my head. Like when ye wake from a deep dream cos theres something not right in the house. I accelerate back to the heath & theres Pignut wi her scarf tied to a bough on the hazel. I dont think shell be able to die in this world. In any world. In fact just as a human straddles the physical world & the other world a fiction lives in two. A fiction lives in the ideas of humans & in that place not affected nor even effected by space & time & thats the secret – philosophers have concentrated on space & time when the vast portion of reality exists outwith that in a place only art can penetrate. The likes of Pignut comes into your world as an idea but you can never come into hers except by short-circuiting spacetime & the mad thing is from a fictions point of view they live in the physical. When theyre alive in your brain its hard to say how theyre different from humans. And where do they go when youre not reading? They wait outside of time & space. Me? Im a different thing altogether. Im a man you dont meet every day.

Oops! Pignuts trying the noose out for size. Not that shell die like I said but it fucks this narrative right up so I grab her away & she tries to speak but were interrupted by Nuncle. Mad old cunts nails are dirty & bleeding wi digging up the Doe. Again. He holds it up to the Great Gods but instead of his usual screaming & ranting he speaks softly he goes An old man, broken with the storms of state, is come to lay his weary bones beside ye; give him a little earth for charity!

Nuncle Tis a naughty night to swim in! I shout an he so-liloquys us hes like I am adrift Boy. Cold air bends the night and stars curve into deep black troughs of my heart where mine soul's but a tiny boat drifting the dark unblinking eye of the universe. I prayed and the Gods ridiculed by crashing waves of desolation. And now the sea falls calm. I have sliced through the broad silver plate of the moon and come to rest upon the soundless belt of Orion. My heart is the all feeling centre of the absolute loneliness of being. No fish, no birds, no wind, no rain. I have failed as king and father. Cordelia is lost & I am nothing now but a husk on a great sea. I float sans time, sans space, sans faith, sans hope. I die then, Boy, a great man humbled.

Nuncle! I scream but he falls on his sword & before I can

reach him theres thunder   lightning & we accelerate down rivers of light…

44

ACT I

SCENE I. King Lears palace

...coming to a stop in a warmer slower place of muffled sounds & scents of feasting. I know exactly where we are & when we are.

Here are the giant flagstones of King Lears plush & abundant court. Were clean & fresh like weve been put through a Hotpoint number four soap sud wash dry press & perfumeation. Three subjects pass in a hurry & bow wi a wee Your Majesty a squint at me & astonishment at Pignut.

Prithee wherefore goest ye in such haste loyal subjects? Nuncle goes & the one wi the black feather looks at him like hes mad & goes Why my Lord to the division of the Kingdom & the woman in red wi the pushed up boobs goes The magnanimity of the most illustrate king shalt honour your memory my good Lord & off they shuffle mutterwhispering.

Joy, Oh Joy! Oh holy Joy! goes Nuncle & grabs me by the cheeks wi both hands Joy boy, Joy to the Gods he goes & plants a full smacker on my lips. & then

& then

& then

as were trying to get our bearings Cordelia passes the corridor end sees her father gives this wee courtesy & goes Sir as gentle as a cloud.

Nuncle stares like shes Holy Mary Mother of God. His eyesre wide & his big beaming smiles unnerving Cordelia. She goes Sir again & a wee mini curtsy a cursette really & off she goes drawing her brows thegether. When her footstepsve diminished Nuncle goes Pignut! Oh Pignut! The air of paradise doth fan the house and angels office all!

He kisses Pignut smack on the lips wi a big Mmmm just as Regan & Goneril pass. Their eyesre like cracked soup plates. Nuncle squints & unsucks his lips from Pignut manages a smile & nods once for each daughter. Both Pelicans lower beaks drop they courtesy go Sir each & shuffle off murmurifying.

& they obviously met Gloucester cos seconds later he comes barrelling round the corner & bellows Ah my liege. My Liege. There you are!

Good Gloucester goes Nuncle wi a joy that hits Gloucester like a smack in the face Come hither let thy King see thee better for closer to a friend is closer to the Gods.

Nuncle holds Gloucester by the shoulders & goes Sir, I am a poor friend of yours, that loves you.

My Lord?

Tis you Nuncle goes Tis really thee Gloucester?

Yes my Lord. Tis I goes Gloucester & throws a questioning

glance at me then a wondering one at Pignut. Nuncle twists Gloucesters head an goes And thine eyes intact?

Eh, yes my Lord.

Let me touch them goes Nuncle & runs his thumbs over Gloucesters eyes. Gloucester winces & stands firm but by his mouth hes uneasy when Nuncle softly kisses each eye in turn & pushes Gloucester away to better look at him.

And this place? Nuncle goes It is my palace?

Is my Lord feeling well?

Well? Feeling well good and loyal Gloucester? Thy Lord is better than ever and happy thine eyes art in good health. Two good eyes.

I had two this morning my Lord when I arithmeticked them he goes & laffs

& Nuncle laffs

& Gloucester laffs more 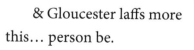 & goes Who might this... person be.

Ah. This is Pignut. She is… she is… she is… & I inbutt Pignut is my apprentice I go.

A female Fool?

Yeah by my decree goes Nuncle A rare talent.

She looketh more the Grim Reaper than a Fool goes Gloucester & laffs & Nuncle goes Pignut hath thy aproof good Gloucester for she maketh thee laff without jest or tumble.

I am happy that thou art so jovial my Lord. Truly I am.

Yeah. And I have good reason to be bright and jovial among my guests this night Gloucester.

And may a lowly Lord enquire why my Lord?

We have been prisoned upon on the stormy heath Nuncle goes but I kick him on the shin like Lucky whacks Estragon in Godot. Nuncle grinsmiles for three seconds too long & into the uneasiness Gloucester goes Your presence is craved in the banqueting hall my Lord. The presence of the King engenders love amongst his subjects and his loyal friends.

We shall be there anon good Gloucester.

You art well prepared my Lord?

Prepared Gloucester?

Ha, your joy has thee forget your duties my Liege. The division of your kingdom!

Ah Nuncle goes Nay, Nay. I shalt have the coming hour o'erflow with joy and pleasure drown the brim. The Gods make this a happy day Gloucester.

Nuncle winks at me & Pignut & Gloucester goes Adieu, be happy & in his walk I see perplexity.

& so in the silence of that corridor Nuncle whispers us his

plan & its great so great so apt so fuckin downright right & radical that Pignut & me laff out loud in the telling.

45

our darker purpofe

Theres a great intake of breath as we pass through the doors. Partly cos Nuncles radiant & partly cos Pignuts weird. Theres murmurs of Shes the Fools apprentice & Shes the Kings consort as the court sets a whispering. Before Nuncle can take his seat busting through the throng come Regan & Goneril each taking a hand & gushing platitudes like two smack starved junkies on the make.

Regan goes Is your dear highness well?

I am in best spirits he goes & shes like I am well pleased, your patience and your virtue well deserves it, Sir & shes practically bumped out the road by Goneril who commandeers both hands & goes Sir, show th' incredulous world the noble changes in thee. I am glad to see you healthfull. I am glad to see you in this merry vein: what means such a smile? I pray you, master, tell me.

And I am a father joyful almost to bursting to have my daughters' company this day. See that ye are fairly seated he goes waves them away & goes Attend to my two Fools that they be seated to my left and right at the table.

Well! Theres an almighty gasp but the orders obeyed & were seated by the King wi the whole court whispering about Pignut. Stuff like Clothes these art not clothes. A woman nay! Hath the King a consort? But Nuncle hears none of this. He has only eyes for Cordelia seated in demure & splendid containment sipping gently from her glass.

Sweet innocence Nuncle goes & Im like Yeah Nuncle thank the Gods.

I do Boy he goes I do. For I have witnessed my errors smothered in carnage.

There goes good Kent, Nuncle I go & Kents shocked when Nuncle gives him a wave you might get from your mate passing on a Glasgow bus. The court downhushes when Kent gives Nuncle the same wave back.

Nuncle lets out this big bellow of a laff.

Then I laff.

Even Pignut laffs.

Then in comes that creepy cunt Edmund. He has trouble walking across the floor cos Nuncle fixes a big cheesy grin on him & just before he reaches Cornwall Edmund trips to the sniggers of the crowd.

The minstrels play the meal is served & all is merry. Regan & Goneril take Nuncles insane joy to be the release of retirement.

The conversation drifts back to Pignut. Courtiers are moving close to better see her. To smell her. To judge the fabric of her clothes. A woman in a yellow gown wi white frills sees the watch & whispers to another who shares it on till its the talk of the hall. Politics move fast & forceful in a court & I see Regan and Goneril tete a tete wi Edmund & Cornwall. I drift close an lift a lug cos a Fools invisible & theyre talking about getting rid of Pignut & her magical ticking eye with which she has obviously bewitched the King.

I relay this to Nuncle & he surreptitiously takes the watch from Pignut holds it in the air & goes Before ye stands the most virtuous gentlewoman that ever nature had praise for creating but the murmurs continue till Nuncle points a craggy finger & goes At the next word: no more of 'who is she' speak, or thy word on the instant is thy condemnation and thy death & silence falls & Nuncle throatclears & goes This all seeing eye shalt tell thy King of further dissent. He places the watch on the table & goes Albany, Meantime we shall express our darker purpose, give me the map there.

Albany hands him a vellum scored into three parts & Nuncles like Know that we have divided in three our kingdom and 'tis our fast intent to shake all cares and business from our age, conferring them on younger strengths while we unburthen'd crawl toward death.

He gets a wee polite court snigger for that. Like the way a congregation laffs at a priests jokes. Regan & Goneril sneak a wee glance at each other. Their seated hearts knocking at their ribs. Then I see a thing I never saw the first time & thats Cordelia furtively wiping a tear.

Our son of Cornwall goes Nuncle & Cornwall steps forward falsesmiles & Nuncle falsesmiles back & Nuncle goes And you, our no less loving son of Albany & assisted by a wee push from Goneril up comes Albany & Nuncles like We have this hour a constant will to publish our daughters' several dowers, that future strife may be prevented now.

& he puts a lot of stress on *future strife*. A lot of stress.

Goneril & Regan force their avaricious grins into smiles. Tight stretched lips. Cordelias face is unchanged cold & true as stone.

Nuncle goes The princes, France and Burgundy, great rivals in our youngest daughter's love, long in our court, have made their amorous sojourn, and here are to be answer'd.

France & Burgandy posh nod each other. The kind of nod you do before a duel like wi one arm across your chest & your bottom lip pushed up.

Cordelias blushes & Nuncle goes Tell me, my daughters, since now we will divest us both of rule, interest of territory, cares of state, which of you shall we say doth love me most?

Regan catches a glance at Goneril & Goneril bites her bottom lip but Cordelia stares dead ahead. Nuncle roars into the electric silence Well!? & they jump to attention except Cordelia & Nuncle goes Which of you shall we say doth love me most? That her deserved bounty may extend where nature doth with merit challenge. Goneril, our eldest-born, speak first & upsteps Goneril shaking so much wi anticipation youd think she was goanny explode in orgasm.

As she speaks Nuncle listens wi big eyes & an unnerving grin.

Sir, goes Goneril unleashing too many teeth I love you more than words can wield the matter; dearer than eye-sight, space, and liberty; beyond what can be valued, rich or rare & Im thinking Jesus Christ this is turning into a love song itll be number one soon & she batters on she goes No less than life, with grace, health, beauty, honour; as much as child e'er loved, or father found; a love that makes breath poor, and speech unable; beyond all manner of so much I love you.

Nuncle claps slow enough to make it mibbi sarcastic but fast enough to make it mibbi sincere. He winks at Pignut & she smiles back & the look on Gonerils face is thunder & you can see if she gets power Pignuts heads getting lopped the

fuck right off.

Thats when Cordelia asides What shall Cordelia do? Love, and be silent & Pignut coughs three short blasts & Nuncle turns & Pignut whispers What shall Cordelia do? Love, and be silent & Nuncle whispers My Cordelia hath said this? & Pignuts like What shall Cordelia do? Love, and be silent she said Sir. Nuncle scrutinises Cordelia & the Lords & Ladies fidget nervous wondering if the whispering is about them. Goneril awaits her inheritance her fingers behind her back wrestling each other. Regan stretches the tension out of her neck. Nuncle lifts the vellum coughs a kingly cough & goes Of all these bounds, even from this line to this, with shadowy forests and with champains rich'd, with plenteous rivers and wide-skirted meads, we make *Gloucester* Lord.

Well! Goneril is a wee vignette in the middle of the courts eruption.

What!? she goes & her mouth stuffed wi vile resentment and bitter disbelief cant close. One side of her top lip lifts like a dug as her eyes swivel to Albany who shrugs in disbelief & by now everybody in the Great Hall is gawking at Gloucester who in turn is staring at the flagstones.

Gloucester, come hither to me goes Nuncle & Gloucesters like Me my Lord?

Come hither good and loyal servant.

Gloucester shuffles to Nuncle & Nuncle goes To thine and thy son Edgar's, and barring Edmund from profit, issue be this perpetual & Gloucester goes I am without words my Lord & Nuncle declares to court See here before ye a man without words but plentiful in courage and loyalty. A man who would search for a friend in the wilderness. Who would risk his life to bring to shelter a good and old friend. Who would have his eyes plucked out with a spoon for his King. Who would lay down his life for a friend.

Its great its fuckin great cos Gloucesters fuckin bamboozled. Poor cunt deserves everything Nuncle is giving him & he doesnt know why. Hell never know why not unless he breaks someday through the barrier.

We have been brothers in our blindness good friend and twins in our tragedies goes Nuncle & Gloucester goes Yes my Lord. Very good my Lord.

We shall speak anon good friend goes Nuncle & Gloucester floats off in a cloud of wonder to the bewildered & hushed congratulations of the court.

An then wi a great sense of dramatic timing Nuncle goes What says our second daughter, our dearest Regan, wife to Cornwall?

& Regan drained of her earlier hope & confidence falters forward like shes walking on ice. She gives it bashful hands clasped & head down till Nuncle shouts Speak! & she coughs into the muted hall & goes Sir, I am made of the self-same metal that my sister is & Nuncle asides to Pignut I am certain you are Pelican & Regans like And prize me at her worth. In my true heart I find she names my very deed of love & Nuncle asides She cannot deign to invent her own love but must borrow her sisters!

Only she comes too short goes Regan That I profess myself an enemy to all other joys, which the most precious square of sense possesses; and find I am alone felicitate in your dear highness' love.

Nuncle does the same clap only this time IMHO a bit too sarcastic cos Regan stumbles & catches Cornwall a fearful glance & just at that Cordelia asides Then poor Cordelia! And yet not so; since, I am sure, my love's more richer than my tongue & Pignut coughs & whispers the self-same to Nuncle & Nuncle whispers back My daughter. My young and lovely daughter & Pignuts like Yes Sir & Nuncle smiles & the Lords & Ladies smile but all the more trepidatious & Nuncle speaks to a space an inch above Regans head he goes To thee and thine hereditary ever remain this ample third of our fair kingdom; no less in space, validity, and pleasure than that conferr'd on Gloucester. Regans sigh of relief is suffocated when Nuncle goes Step forward noble Earl of Kent.

The court gasps like a gust of wind & Kent points at himself & Nuncle nods aye & Kent steps up to the throne. Nuncle hands him the vellum & proclaims This man is my most loyal servant. This gallant knave would sit i' the stocks all night for his King. Go in disguise among cutthroats and robbers to protect his King. Bring the King to shelter in a storm. Follow over hill, over dale, thorough bush, thorough brier, over park, over pale, thorough flood, thorough fire. If the King died this man would die with him by his own hand. Here stands an honest man whos counsel I will take forthwith. One third of my kingdom is thine good Caius.

Caius my Lord? goes Kent & Nuncle laffs & goes Apologies good and loyal Kent.

Kent passes through the quiet court & stands by Gloucester. The compass of attention has swung to them. But it soon recalculates & swings back to Cordelia. Who will get her share of the lands? It could be any one of them. The main contenders whisper wi their wives and puff up to better catch the eye of the King.

Real love forged in adversity bursts out of Nuncles face when he goes Now, our joy, although the last, not least; to whose young love the vines of France and milk of Burgundy strive to be interess'd; what can you say to draw a third more opulent than Kent and Gloucester's?

Cordelia downtilts her head takes a breath uptilts & jesus fuck ye can see the love emanating from her eyes. Fuck knows how Nuncle never seen that before. Nuncle goes Speak & Cordelias like Nothing, my Lord & Nuncle goes Nothing? & shes like Nothing, my Lord & he goes Speak again & Cordelia goes Unhappy that I am, I cannot heave my heart into my mouth: I love your majesty according to my bond; nor more nor less & the Lords & Ladies take a sigh of horrorification cos surely her fate will be worse than that of the poetic Pelicans.

How, now, Cordelia! Nuncle goes Continue your speech a little, that it may gather your fortunes.

Good my Lord she goes You have begot me, bred me,

loved me: I return those duties back as are right fit, obey you, love you, and most honour you. Why have my sisters husbands, if they say they love you all? Haply, when I shall wed, that Lord whose hand must take my plight shall carry half my love with him, half my care and duty: Sure, I shall never marry like my sisters, to love my father all.

And goes thy heart with this? Nuncle goes & shes like Ay, good my Lord & hes like So young, and so tender.

So young, my Lord, and true she goes & a smile beams across Nuncles dish & he goes Let it be so then & lifts a gentle hand & goes Now Cordelia! Come hither to your father.

Theres a shake a shift a jolt in time space & reality. The Lords & Ladies check their feet like the ground has moved & then the walls & the roof to see if their world it still intact.

Its not.

Nuncle has veered off course & the whole tragedy is reset. Fear must go somewhere & it goes a ripping through the hall. Eyes bulge hearts race sweaty palms grasp others mouths become vast droughted deserts.

Nuncle surprises Cordelia by the ferocity of his embrace & she lightkisses his cheek & goes I love you father. Nuncle releases his grief in a great cry that shakes the world & a tear rolls from his cheek & splashes on the flagstone making a sound no one will ever hear. Then he laffs a laff Ive never heard from man nor beast kisses Cordelia & kisses her again again again & goes And your father loves sweet Cordelia & shes like Good my Lord & Nuncle strokes her skinwhite cheek & deep into her eyes he looks & goes So young, and so wise

& he pulls her again to his breast & asides to Pignut I thank heaven for you. You burst the future open good Pignut.

Pignut bows & goes My Lord, my King & Nuncle stands & takes Cordelia by the wrist raises her hand like a boxers & goes Hear ye. Hear ye Lords and Ladies & when quiet falls he bellows I sparkle in the spirits of my daughter. Behold Queen Cordelia. This fair Queen shall rule over the three portions of the kingdom.

Regan rushes forwards spitting saliva from her mouth What about me, what about my portion! Goneril sinks to her knees & scream Father, morsel us, do not leave us destitute.

Let this be so; thy lies, Pelicans, be thy dower Nuncle goes For, by the sacred radiance of the sun, the mysteries of Hecate, and the night; by all the operation of the orbs from whom we do exist, and cease to be; here I disclaim all my paternal care, propinquity and property of blood, and as a stranger to my heart and me hold thee, and thee from this, for ever. The barbarous Scythian, or he that makes his generation messes to gorge his appetite, shall to my bosom be as well neighbour'd, pitied, and relieved, as thee and thee my sometime daughters.

They try to reason but Nuncle holds up a hand silences them & goes The Gods to their dear shelter take thee, maids, that justly think'st, and hast most rightly said!

Father goes Cordelia but hes like Tis your choice to bring back these Pelicans to court should you see fit change in their souls.

Yes my Lord.

Gods bless the Queen goes Nuncle & kisses Queen Cordelia on the forehead lets out this great roar of a laff & Light-

ning cracks

the walls fall away the players tumble into mist & the moon reveals the heath, the tree and the stones.

returned to the heath (10)

& standing alone
abandoned
Pignut
I watch from my hiding place & truth be told I feel big
sorrow for our Pignut. It takes a few stunned seconds but
when she realises where she is she screams No! No! No!

She crouches muttering something I cant hear then suddenly runs full pelt into the whistling storm.

& is flung instanter back.

She tries again landing on her arsebone & shouts Is this
my reward for a season of exertion? Is this my reward... &
she bewilders & goes For... for the instances that occurred?
She teethgrits & goes Awake! Jane Eyre - awake! & she slaps
her face & despite Foolrules Im about to go to her aid but a

SUPERSIZZLE

Pins me to the dark.

Then footsteps.

Im thinking forfucksakes let this not be Nuncle let this not be Lear. Canny do this whole thing again. My foolish heart couldnt take it.

Pignut hears the footsteps & goes Sir? Nuncle, Lear, is that you?

The footsteps don't answer & she goes Mister Fool? Are you there?

I cant answer & then this absolutely stunning girl wi long black hair pops out the storm & comes to a jolting halt when she sees Pignut & goes Have they come for me? & Pignuts like Pardon? & the girl goes Have they come for me miss? & Pignuts like Has who come for you? & the girl goes If they have I be almost glad, yes, glad!

May I ask who you are, miss? goes Pignut & the girl her eyes focussed on some past deed goes It is as it should be. This happiness could not have lasted. It was too much. Where be this place miss? & Pignuts like This is, this is, we are on a moor, a heath, of whose geography I am not exactly certain.

The girl points back to where she came from & goes I have just come from… but Pignut goes I am afraid you may be trapped, for I fear I am.

Trapped miss? Goes the beautiful girl & Pignuts like Yes. I have been trapped here for days or weeks… I don't know how long I've been trapped. I am unable to leave & then she stops & goes Did you meet anyone?

No one miss.

A King and a Fool, perhaps?

The girls attention is piqued & she goes Who are you miss?

Who am I? goes Pignut & the girl goes Yes miss. You speak in a strange Northern accent so I be wondering who you are & Pignut looks at the heather then at the girl & goes I have a less definite notion of my identity than before, miss.

But do you have a name miss? she goes & Pignuts like Yes, please accept my apologies for being so impolite, my name is Jane, Jane Eyre & the girl gives her this funny look & Pignuts like Why do you look at me thus? & the girl goes Your name be Jane Eyre?

Yes goes Pignut & the girl repeats the look & Pignuts like Have I said something wrong?

The girl goes Jane Eyre be the name of a lady from a book, miss, a novel, that's all & Pignuts like It is a book I have never heard of & the girl goes Jane Eyre be a character in this novel. Jane Eyre be the very name of this novel.

Jane Eyre is the title of a novel? goes Pignut & the girls like Yes miss, Jane Eyre written by Charlotte Bronte?

Bronte?

Charlotte Bronte.

I am not acquainted with a writer by the name of Charlotte Bronte.

I have read it once miss. Being not much of a reader, though, it took me a while. But you have been named for her? I'm thinking, your accent being northern, your parents may have read it.

Where have you come from? goes Pignut & the girls like

Stonehenge, I thinks miss & looks around like shes lost her way & Pignut goes I must have travelled a long way & the girls like A long way from where, miss? & Pignut goes Thornton Hall.

The girl takes a step back & goes That be the name of the hall in the Jane Eyre novel. That be where Mister Rochester abides & Pignut blurts out Rochester? Have you seen Mr Rochester?

I think I should like to leave goes the girl & Pignut grabs her shoulders & goes Have you seen Mister Rochester.

No, no!

What the devil have you seen then!?

The girl screams & breaks free & steps into the storm but is flung back on her lovely arse. There was tragedy in her eyes before but now theres also fear.

I be walking days & nights she goes And you are still here miss & she crawls backwards & Pignut goes You can't leave but the girl screams & runs full tilt & is sent full tilt back even more terrified & goes Please Jane Eyre... if you be a witch... a Jane Eyre come alive! Please do not harm me.

Pignut goes Shh Shh! but the girl backcrawls more Please! she goes My life be cursed enough with ill luck and untoward omens, have mercy & Pignuts like Be calm.

Stay back spirit of Jane Eyre!

I won't hurt you.

I have a knife the girl goes I have already killed a man & Pignut uppalms & goes I shall not take another step & the girls like You had better not & Pignut goes Could I inquire as to your name, miss?

Why do you wish my name? she goes & Pignuts like Out of common politeness just as you asked my name earlier & the girls like There are people looking for me on account of what I did miss.

If there are people looking for you, I can assure you, miss, that they won't find you here.

No miss?

No. This is a place one doesn't pass by every day, no one will find you here goes Pignut & smiles & the girl smiles uneasily & Pignut goes Tell me your name.

My name be Tess.

And do you have a surname Tess?

Yes miss. My full name be Tess Durbyfield, some speak it D'Urberville miss, in the French fashion.

The robin lands & chirps. Thunder strikes & lightning flashes & I am back at Nuncles banquet & at the top of the table sits good Cordelia & her smile is radiant.

Further Reading

The Promise
When promises can cost lives

Simon's Wife
Time is running out, and history is
being rewritten by a traitor's hand.

The Unforgiven King
A forgotten woman and the
most vilified king in history

American Goddess
Ancient powers
and new forces

L. M. Affrossman

Science for Heretics
Why so much of science is wrong

The Tethered God
Punished for a crime he can't
remember

Barrie Condon

Pignut and Nuncle
When we are born, we cry that
we have come to this stage of fools
King Lear

Des Dillon

Two Pups
What makes us different.
What makes us the same.

Seona Calder

Drown for your Sins
DCI Grant McVicar: Book 1

Dress for Death
DCI Grant McVicar: Book 2

Diarmid MacArthur

Comics and Columbine
An outcast look at comics, big-
otry and school shootings

Tom Campbell

www.sparsilebooks.com